D0837874

'WHO ASKED YOU TO BILL IN?'

Waco was watching every move. The five men were set on trouble, that he was sure of. He was also sure that he could not sit by and watch the girl cut down.

'Hold it!'

Waco's warning came as he pushed back his chair and stood up, facing the five men. They turned their attention to this new factor in the game, eyes taking in every detail of his dress and armament. Waco stood without moving, allowing the men to look, his hands by the matched, staghorn grips of his Colts, ready to move and turn all hell loose.

'Who asked you to bill in?' Kyte asked.

'I'm in, likewise I'm asking you to leave peaceable and let me eat my food.'

'Yeah?' sneered Kyte, glancing at the others. 'Well, I ...'

'I requested it,' Waco drawled evenly. 'Hereby I demonstrates.'

The crowd let out a concerted gasp. The five men stood without a movement, froze fast and solid. Waco's hands had moved, and how they'd moved. The matched guns were out, the five-and-a-half-inch barrels lining on the men.

Books by J. T. Edson Arranged in chronological order

Ole Devil Hardin Stories
YOUNG OLE DEVIL
OLE DEVIL AND THE CAPLOCKS †
GET URREA *

Civil War Stories
COMANCHE
YOU'RE IN COMMAND NOW, MR. FOG
THE BIG GUN
UNDER THE STARS AND BARS
THE FASTEST GUN IN TEXAS
KILL DUSTY FOG!
THE DEVIL GUN
THE COLT AND THE SABRE
THE REBEL SPY
THE BLOODY BORDER
BACK TO THE BLOODY BORDER

The Floating Outfit Stories
THE YSABEL KID
.44 CALIBRE MAN
A HORSE CALLED MOGOLLON
GOODNIGHT'S DREAM
FROM HIDE AND HORN
SET TEXAS BACK ON HER FEET
THE HIDE AND TALLOW MEN
THE HOODED RIDERS
QUIET TOWN
TRAIL BOSS
WAGONS TO BACKSIGHT
TROUBLED RANGE
SIDEWINDER
RANGELAND HERCULES
MCGRAW'S INHERITANCE
THE HALF-BREED
THE WILDCATS
THE BAD BUNCH
THE FAST GUN
CUCHILO
A TOWN CALLED YELLOWDOG
TRIGGER FAST
THE MAKING OF A LAWMAN
THE TROUBLE BUSTERS
THE LAW OF THE GUN
THE PEACEMAKERS
TO ARMS, TO ARMS, IN DIXIE!
HELL IN THE PALO DURO
GO BACK TO HELL
THE SOUTH WILL RISE AGAIN
SET A-FOOT †
THE RUSHERS
THE QUEST FOR BOWIE'S BLADE
THE FORTUNE HUNTERS
THE HARD RIDERS
THE RIO HONDO KID
WACO'S DEBT
THE TEXAN
THE FLOATING OUTFIT
APACHE RAMPAGE
RIO GUNS
RIO HONDO WAR
GUNSMOKE THUNDER

THE MAN FROM TEXAS
GUN WIZARD
THE SMALL TEXAN
THE TOWN TAMERS
RETURN TO BACKSIGHT
TERROR VALLEY
GUNS IN THE NIGHT

Waco Stories
SAGEBRUSH SLEUTH
ARIZONA RANGER
WACO RIDES IN
THE DRIFTER
DOC LEROY M.D. †
HOUND-DOG MAN

Calamity Jane Series
COLD DECK, HOT LEAD
CALAMITY SPELLS TROUBLE
TROUBLE TRAIL
THE BULL WHIP BREED
THE COW THIEVES
WHITE STALLION, RED MARE
THE WHIP AND THE WAR LANCE †
THE BIG HUNT

John Slaughter Stories
SLAUGHTER'S WAY
SLAUGHTER'S NEIGHBOURS †

Brady Anchor and Jefferson Trade Stories
TWO MILES TO THE BORDER
WHO DO YOU TRUST, UNCLE BRADY? †

Waxahachie Smith Stories
NO FINGER ON THE TRIGGER †
SLIP GUN
WAXAHACHIE SMITH †
CURE THE TEXAS FEVER †

Rockabye County Stories
SIXTEEN DOLLAR SHOOTER
THE SHERIFF OF ROCKABYE COUNTY †
THE PROFESSIONAL KILLERS
THE ⅛ SECOND DRAW
THE DEPUTIES
POINT OF CONTACT
THE OWLHOOT
RUN FOR THE BORDER
BAD HOMBRE
THEY CALL IT PROGRESS †

The School Swot Stories Written in collaboration with Peter Clawson
BLONDE GENIUS

Bunduki Series
BUNDUKI
BUNDUKI AND DAWN *

† In preparation   * Awaiting publication
and published by CORGI BOOKS

THE DRIFTER

CORGI BOOKS
A DIVISION OF TRANSWORLD PUBLISHERS LTD

THE DRIFTER

A CORGI BOOK 552 07845 x

Originally published in Great Britain
by Brown Watson, Ltd.

PRINTING HISTORY
Corgi Edition published 1968
Corgi Edition reprinted 1969
Corgi Edition reprinted 1972
Corgi Edition reprinted 1975

Copyright © 1963 by Brown Watson, Ltd.
Copyright © 1968 by Transworld Publishers, Ltd.

This book is set in
Baskerville 9 on 10½ pt.

Corgi Books are published by Transworld Publishers, Ltd.
Cavendish House, 57–59 Uxbridge Road, Ealing,
London, W.5.

Made and printed in Great Britain by
Richard Clay (The Chaucer Press), Ltd., Bungay, Suffolk

CHAPTER ONE

ELLA BAKER'S SALOON

THE first thing Waco saw as he entered the Twin Bridge Saloon in the town of Two Forks, Utah Territory, was the complete lack of male help. The saloon was large, spacious, clean looking; but behind the polished mahogany bar, waiting on the tables, handling the dealing at the faro, vingt-un and chuck-a-luck layouts were girls. The only two men who worked in the place were never, or only rarely, seen in business hours, they were a couple of stove-up old cowhands who were employed as swampers.

If Waco was looking around him with interest, the occupants of the saloon were giving him their attention in return. They saw a tall, wide-shouldered, blond-haired, handsome young Texas cowhand. It showed in his low-crowned, wide-brimmed, expensive Stetson hat, which was pushed back from the curly blond hair. The face was tanned, young looking and handsome. It was a strong face, the blue eyes meeting a man's without flinching, the mouth firm yet looking as if it would smile easily. Around his throat was knotted a scarlet silk bandana which hung long ends almost to the waistband of his brown levis, over his dark blue shirt. On his feet were star-decorated, high-heeled, made-to-measure boots with Kelly spurs. Around his waist was a brown leather buscadero gun-belt and in the holsters reposed a matched brace of staghorn-butted Colt Artillery Peacemakers. The holsters told a tale to a man who knew the West. This young man wore the clothing of a tophand of the cattle business, but the two holsters were those of a real fast man with a gun. They were cut to the contours of the guns, leaving clear and easy access to the trigger guards of the revolvers and flaring the butts out so as to be easily lifted clear. The tips of the holsters were tied down, another sign.

He moved from the door, sitting at an empty table and looking up at the pretty girl-waiter who came to him. She ignored his look and stared pointedly at a large sign on the wall over the door. Waco followed her gaze, reading: 'CHECK YOUR GUNS HERE.'

'Why I tell you, ma'am,' he said, his voice a pleasant Texas drawl. 'Was I to take 'em off I'd surely get so light I'd float away. That being so I'll take me the cowhand special.'

The girl made no attempt to move, her eyes went to the two women who stood by the bar.

Ella Baker, a medium-sized woman in her late thirties, stood at the bar talking with her daughter Lynn and watched the by-play between the waitress and Waco. Folks in Two Forks wondered why Ella ran a saloon, but did not complain, for she kept an honest house. She was a good-looking woman, her shapely figure emphasised by a green satin dress.

While Lynn Baker owned girl's clothing, she rarely wore it. A scarlet silk bandana trailed its ends over a black male shirt which tucked into blue jeans that showed off a slim, but shapely figure. Boyishly short black hair framed a pretty, tanned face which never felt cosmetics. Around her waist hung a gunbelt with a pearl-handled Colt Lightning ·41 revolver in its cross-draw holster.

The reason for Lynn's skill with a gun and her wearing men's clothing most of the time came from being brought up by her father on a ranch in Wyoming. Ella and her husband separated soon after Lynn was born, the husband keeping Lynn on in the wild Hole in the Wall country, where she lived the life of a boy rather than a girl.

Before Lynn's father died he wrote to Ella, who sent for Lynn to come along and live with her. Lynn did not wish to, but her friends insisted she did so. Lynn joined her mother in the thriving town of Two Forks and now, after six months, was completely devoted to the woman she could barely remember.

Ella caught the signal from the waitress but before she could reply, Lynn gave an angry snort.

'The nerve of that drifter,' she snorted angrily. 'I'll soon make him hand over his guns.'

6

'No, let it ride!' Ella replied, voice low and urgent. 'He's not just a dressed-up cowhand. He's one of the good guns.'

'I've seen better,' answered Lynn. 'We can't——'

Ella's hand caught her daughter's arm, holding it. Her voice grew harder as she snapped, 'Stop it, Lynn! I said cut it out!'

In the early days of their association Lynn tried to rebel against her mother's will; but only once. The memory of the thrashing it brought her remained long after the ache had left Lynn's saddle-toughened seat. Lynn learned her lesson that day and, strangely, was more devoted and respectful to her mother after it.

Lynn felt surprised at her mother's attitude. Usually Ella insisted that the gun-checking rule be carried out and Lynn could see no reason why the Texan rated different treatment.

The batwing doors of the saloon were thrown open and five men trooped in. They were clearly on the prod and Ella felt scared. Before she could say a word to prevent her daughter moving, Lynn was crossing the room towards the men.

The five stood inside the doors, a tall dark-haired, hand-some gambler in the centre, his coat shoved back to expose the black gunbelt with the rosewood-handled, nickelled Colt in the gunfighter's holster. At his right stood a tall, good-looking, dandy-dressed youngster wearing range clothes and with a low-tied Colt at his side. At the other side stood a short, swarthy man wearing dude clothes; a sly and vicious-looking man. The other two were typical hired guns, the kind who would sell their Colts and such loyalty as they felt necessary, to the highest bidder and stay fairly loyal until the pay no longer came.

'All right, Matt Kyte,' Lynn said. 'Check your guns in.'

The gambler threw back his head and laughed. 'You hear that, boys?' he whooped. 'A dame in pants giving *men* orders.'

'Yeah,' leered the young gunhand. 'Only we ain't taking them. See, girlie, we're tired of taking orders from a skirt.'

'That's right,' went on the small dude. 'Ole Matt here says we should go for a drink.'

'Sure you can,' Lynn agreed. 'We wouldn't stop even you drinking here. But you check your guns first and you behave.'

'Behave, huh?' Kyte grunted, then nodded to one of the gunmen who kicked a chair over. 'You mean like that?'

7

The customers and the girls were watching, ready to get under cover, for they knew Lynn was not the sort to take this treatment. Ella, face pale, moved along the bar and without needing to be told what to do, Molly, biggest of the bartenders, lifted the Merwin and Hullbert revolver and laid it on the bar top, sliding it to Ella, then lifting out a sawed-off shotgun.

'You'd best get out, Kyte,' Lynn warned, her hand lifting towards her belt.

'There she goes again,' Kyte snorted. 'Ordering folks about. The gunbelt makes her think she's a man. We'll have to treat her like one.'

Waco was watching every move. The five men were set on trouble, that he was sure of. He was also sure that he could not sit by and watch the girl cut down. Then Waco's eyes narrowed, he saw the gambler lift a hand, it brushed against the butt of the gun, pushing down slightly, then lifted to hover the gun butt. It was then Waco knew he must cut in and help. The girl looked capable enough but she did not know the danger she was in.

'Hold it!'

Waco's warning came as he pushed back his chair and stood up, facing the five men. They turned their attention to this new factor in the game, eyes taking in every detail of his dress and armament. Waco stood without moving, allowing the men to look, his hands hung by the matched, staghorn grips of his Colts, ready to move and turn all hell loose.

'Who asked you to bill in?' Kyte asked.

'I'm in, likewise I'm asking you to leave peaceable and let me eat my food.'

'Yeah?' sneered Kyte, glancing at the others. 'Well, I——'

'I requested it,' Waco drawled evenly. 'Hereby I demonstrates.'

The crowd let out a concerted gasp. The five men stood without a movement, frozen fast and solid. Waco's hands had moved, and how they'd moved. The matched guns were out, the five-and-a-half-inch barrels lining on the men.

There was not a move from Kyte's bunch; the young gunman had begun what he fondly imagined to be a fast draw, but now stood with his hands a scant half inch from his gun butt. The others were not making a move, they'd no intention of doing so. A man did not learn to draw as fast as that without attaining a considerable accuracy in calling his shots after the draw.

'That, gentlemen,' the soft-drawled voice went on, 'is the third fastest draw in Texas.'

Staring at Waco in admiration, Lynn suddenly realised this was the man she spoke so airily of disarming on his arrival.

For a moment Kyte's eyes met those of the Texan, then he looked down at the floor again, and growled, 'Who asked you to cut in?'

'Just say I'm a hide-bound natural horner-inner,' answered Waco. 'I'm in, gambling man, and in I stay. Unless you and your four brave *amigos* want to take me out again.' There did not appear to be any great delight at this offer so Waco went on, 'Lift your hand, gambling man.' He saw the eager glint in Kyte's eyes and punctured his pleasure at birth. 'Do it fast or slow and I'll *string* along.'

The words hit Kyte hard, especially the way one of them was emphasised. A look of hate and anger crossed his face. The Texan knew his ace in the hole, knew it, could copper the bet and call 'keno' at the end of it. The gun in the trick holster was still a good bet for a man to call on, all it needed was the sense to back the play to the end. If he started to use the gun he would have to back it to the end. Kyte knew that he could see no sign of worry or indecision on the young Texan's face.

Slowly Kyte started to lift his hand. The other men tensed for they knew the secret of the trick holster. They were ready to back Kyte if he called the play but were leaving it to him.

Lynn stood watching; she saw Kyte's hands lift. Suddenly the gun kicked up out of the holster and started to fall towards the floor, only to be arrested by a thin black cord which was looped around the gun-butt and invisible against the black of his jacket. She gasped, this was a trick she'd never seen or heard of before and one which would have taken her by surprise.

'There's a spring in the bottom of the holster,' Waco said, seeing the amazement on the girl's face. 'I figgered you didn't know that one.'

Kyte stood still, face working in rage. The trick holster was costly and now the secret was out he could never rely on it again. His temper made him snarl out a threat at the man who had humiliated him.

'You'll be sorry you cut in, drifter!'

Waco's right-hand Colt roared, the cord suspending Kyte's gun was cut and the rosewood-handled Colt started to fall. Before it hit the floor, Waco's left-hand Colt crashed, kicking back against his palm, the bullet smashing Kyte's Colt in mid-air and knocking it across the room. Then, almost before the Colt hit the floor, Waco's matched guns whirled on his fingers and went back into leather.

'Like the lady said,' he drawled. 'Either check the guns or leave.'

Although the four men looked to their leader for guidance, he gave them none. Kyte's boss did not care for failure, but the gunman had no way of carrying out his orders. Turning, he walked towards the door and the others followed.

Waco grinned at Lynn, looking about fifteen years old as he did. 'Reckon I could have a meal now, ma'am?' he asked. 'Without checking my guns?'

Lynn chuckled, there was admiration in her eyes. 'Sure, it's on the house.'

Ella Baker looked thoughtful, studying Waco with interest. She slid the gun along the bar top and without even looking Molly caught it, placed it and the shotgun under the counter, then went on serving.

Waco was just sitting down when Ella walked towards him. He pushed back his chair and came to his feet politely. 'Thanks,' she said. 'I'm the owner of this place. Lynn's my daughter. May we join you?'

'Be my pleasure, ma'am,' Waco replied, pulling Ella a chair out. Lynn took her own, kicking her leg over the back and sitting down as if mounting a horse.

Ella noticed the young man did not offer his name, not even after she introduced herself and Lynn to him. She made no attempt to get his name for she'd a shrewd idea who he was and what he was doing here. She offered him a drink but he refused, saying he wanted a meal, and was then going to find work.

'You said the third fastest double draw in Texas,' she said, checking her suspicions as to his identity. 'Who're the other two?'

'Dusty Fog and Mark Counter, ma'am.'

'Are you staying in town?' she asked.

'No, ma'am, a man likes to try eating regular and I'm not overlong on cash. I allowed to head out and get me a riding chore.'

'The town needs a lawman,' Ella remarked. 'A good man. There's an election for sheriff in a fortnight. The right man could get in.'

'Sure, ma'am. I'm not known hereabouts and not likely to get known.'

Ella did not reply for a moment. She glanced at the barroom, her girls were busy working among the customers who were in at this early hour. Then she studied Waco again. The visit from Matt Kyte warned her that she'd almost left things too late, only this young Texan being here prevented a tragic shooting.

'The last place anyone would think of looking for you would be handling the law in a wide open town like this,' she remarked casually. 'Especially if you didn't use your own name. I could help you get known and I think you'd make the kind of lawman I want.'

Waco took his makings from his vest pocket and rolled a smoke, offering Lynn the sack but she declined. With his smoke going, Waco gave the matter his thought. He needed work, but also needed to keep out of sight for a few more weeks. The Pinkertons were looking for Waco, Captain Mosehan and Doc Leroy.*

The handling of the law in a town like Two Forks was something he was qualified to do. He'd learnt his trade under Dusty Fog in Mulrooney, Kansas, and finished his education as an Arizona Ranger. However, there was something he needed to be sure of before he took on. The answer to the next question would tell him if he should or should not take the job.

'I learned me a rule from Dusty Fog,' he said. 'Never take money from two sets of folk. If I take on as law I don't take sides or play any favourites.'

*Reason is told in *Waco Rides In* by J. T. Edson.

'Which is just what I want. You know more than a little about crooked gambling, I hear. My games are open to your inspection at any time. I don't need a man of mine in office, but I do need a fair man. There is only one other candidate for office, Von Schnabel. If he gets in I won't last a week here.'

'He's that big?' inquired Waco mildly.

'He runs the Guesthouse across the street from here. Those were five of his men who just came in. And he's got the backing of every crooked grafter in town.'

'Which same being a fair piece of backing for one man,' said Waco dryly. 'How do you stand with the town?'

'Pretty well. I was one of the earliest settlers, ran this place before the boom came. There are a lot of decent folks who want to see the town cleaned up. I could hold Von Schnabel but there's the floating vote, the fence-sitters who'll go for the man they think best suited. With what I know of you, and what I could to help they'd go for you.'

A man entered the saloon and came to the table. 'Hear about Von Schnabel, Miss Ella?' he asked. 'Had him a falling out with Matt Kyte and four more of his men, turned them out, fired them.'

'When was this?' asked Waco.

'Early this morning,' replied the man, then headed for the bar.

'Handy,' grunted Waco. 'He fires them in the morning, afore they come here causing trouble. I'll give her a whirl, Miss Ella, ma'am.'

'That's the boy,' said Ella delightedly. 'Bix Smith and Simon Girty are the two deputies. They'll take you on if I give them the word.'

'That's what I need, ma'am,' Waco replied, smiling. 'Some real good help. I don't want my name mentioning though.'

'I'll see to it. That trouble just now, what do you make of it?'

'Nothing much yet,' answered Waco. 'It could be they did get fired and were feeling mean; came here to cause trouble and get their boss in bad.'

'It could be that,' Ella agreed. 'Kyte's a mean man at the best of times. I think that——'

Whatever Ella thought was never said. From outside she heard a wild yell and the crash of shots followed by the tinkling of broken glass. Then came another wild yell and more shots. The sound came from one of the two streets which joined in front of the Two Bridge Saloon.

'Just a drunk,' Ella said, shrugging. 'That's one of the things which a good lawman would be able to stop. Bix and Simon could and probably would.'

The sound of the shots came nearer and Waco pushed back his chair, taking up his hat. He set the hat on, then automatically saw to the hang of his guns. 'I'll come back for the meal, ma'am,' he said.

'It might not be——' Ella began, then stopped.

Waco was not listening to her. He was walking towards the doors of the saloon. Outside there sounded more shots, getting closer to the saloon all the time.

CHAPTER TWO

DRIFTER SMITH, FROM TEXAS

Two Forks lay just above the junction of the Colorado and San Juan Rivers. A bridge crossed each river, it having been found easier to span the two smaller water-courses than the combined stream.

Ella's saloon was the first building, laying at the tip of the Y shape made by the two rivers. Facing Ella's Twin Bridge Saloon lay the Guesthouse, owned by a German called Kurt Von Schnabel. The rest of the town stretched along the two main streets, one running parallel to either river. Along Colorado Street and San Juan Street ran the business section of the town, almost half of which was saloons, dance-halls, gambling houses. There also were the theatre and the jail.

It was a rough town, a hard town, a town in need of a strong lawman. The sheriff of Two Forks County was popularly supposed to be making a tax collection around the county and his two old deputies did what they could, but it was a job for more than two men.

The need for strong law-enforcement became apparent as Ben Wharton reeled down Colorado Street. Stockily-built, long-haired, wearing smoke-blackened buckskins and Sioux moccasins, his two Cavalry Peacemakers augmented by a saw-edged bowie knife sheathed at his belt and an Arkansas toothpick thrust down the top of one calf-high moccasin, he made an awe-inspiring sight. While there were men in town who could have quietened Wharton with ease, none wished to chance it against a man as drunk as he.

'I'm Ben Wharton!' he screeched while reloading his guns. 'I'm so pizen mean that if a snake bites me he up and dies. When I howl grizzly b'ars turn white and when I spit the ground boils up. This's my night to howl!'

Not a bad performance considering he took only one drink before starting out to terrorise the town. Deciding that Kyte would have dealt with Lynn Baker, Wharton headed for the Twin Bridge Saloon. With Lynn out of the way, Wharton reckoned he could play out the next part of his employer's plan easily enough.

A tall young man left the Twin Bridge Saloon, paused to stroke the neck of a big paint stallion standing at the hitching rail, then walked across the street in Wharton's direction.

Dust kicked up under Waco's heels as he went towards Wharton, never taking his eyes from the other man even though he knew many people watched him.

Gone was the cheerful cowhand, replaced by Waco the lawman; the lightning-fast fighting machine raised on the wild Texas plains, brought forth on the cattle trails, maturing as deputy marshal under Dusty Fog in Mulrooney,* and reaching its peak as an Arizona Ranger.†

A memory shocked Wharton and brought him to a halt. He remembered seeing another cowhand, in a small Texas town, striding towards him in that same purposeful manner. Only backing down and eating crow had saved Wharton on that occasion. Then Wharton tried to comfort himself with the thought that the man now approaching him was no more than a dressed-up show-off button trying to act tough.

'Outa my way, boy!' Wharton yelled, but his guns' barrels sagged groundwards. 'I'm a roaring river and busting my banks.'

Waco neither replied nor broke his stride. Watching Wharton's hands, he prepared to draw and shoot should the barrels start to rise. All the time Waco kept remembering Dusty Fog's advice for handling such a situation: 'A drunk will always stop when his eyes focus on you. Move in closer and you throw him off balance.' As Dusty's advice mostly proved correct, Waco let Wharton halt, then advanced three more strides.

'What you wanting, boy?' asked Wharton, his voice no longer tough.

'Your guns,' Waco replied, locking Wharton's eyes with his own.

*Told in *The Trouble Busters*.
†Told in *Sagebrush Sleuth* and *Arizona Ranger*.

Wharton tried to stare Waco down, and failed. 'You want my guns?'

'You're not deaf, mister. Hand them over!'

'You the law in town?' asked Wharton, hoping to bluff long enough for help to come.

'Just a citizen doing my public duty, mister. Making a citizen's arrest, as is my right granted in our grand 'n' glorious Constitution. Which same allows us to do anything we aren't stopped from doing by the law.'

'Who are you?'

There Waco was stuck for a moment. He did not want his own name to be mentioned around the town. Then he had an inspiration, something Kyte had called him. 'The name's Drifter Smith, from Texas,' he drawled easily. 'Now how about those guns?'

'You figger you can take my guns?' he asked.

'*You* figger I can't?' was the mocking reply.

Waco's hand lifted, going up to shove his hat back slightly. Wharton tensed, for he knew that few men ever learned to use a gun with the left hand. This could be the chance he was waiting for. Then another thought hit him, a thought which froze his hand to his side. Would any man take a chance like that unless he was fast, if not faster with his left hand gun? Wharton knew he would not and judged everyone by his own low standards.

When Wharton failed to take advantage of his move, Waco knew he'd won. The time was on hand to finish the play, to call Wharton and see his hand.

'Toss those guns down here at my feet!' snapped Waco, his voice hard and decisive. 'I'm waiting!'

Wharton's hands went to the butts of his guns. There was a scattering for cover from the watching people but Waco never moved, never took his eyes from the other man's face.

The watching crowd scattered hurriedly to hunt for cover, expecting shooting to commence. Even though he held his guns in his hands, Wharton could not raise the courage to make a play. Giving a long shudder, he tossed the guns to the ground at Waco's feet.

'Now the knives,' Waco went on.

Eager questions ran among the spectators as Wharton dis-

carded his knives. Those who overheard Waco introduce himself to Wharton passed on the name. That was Drifter Smith,
from Texas! Maybe not his real name, but none felt willing to
challenge the Texan on the issue.

'All right,' Waco said as he bent to pick up the weapons.
'You can collect these from the jail when you're ready to pay
for the damage you've done. Now drift and do it *pronto*!'

Wharton turned on his heel, slinking off behind the Guesthouse out of sight. Waco hefted the weapons he held and
turned to a man who was near to him.

'Where'd a man find the jail, happen he wanted to?' he
asked.

'Round on San Juan Street, Drifter,' the man replied. 'That
was some slick work there, ain't never seen it done better.'

'Or me!' whooped another man. 'Yes, sir, Drifter. You sure
made him crawl in his hole and pull the top down.'

Waco nodded his acknowledgement to the compliments. A
whistle brought his paint to him—the horse had been trained
to stand still without needing tying. He swung into the saddle
and rode along San Juan Street in search of the jail. Even
before Waco reached his destination, men took news into the
Twin Bridges Saloon of how Drifter Smith disarmed a bad-
mean drunk and heard in return that the same man faced
down Matt Kyte and his four friends.

The sheriff's office and jail was a large single storey, but
strongly made stone building. Waco left his horse at the hitching rail and entered the big front door. A couple of old-timers
were playing cribbage at the desk when he entered, neither of
them even looking up. Waco took a moment to examine his
surroundings and study the two old deputies.

If the deputies had been one type of lawman he would have
left the weapons and backed out of the deal right away. He
liked what he saw. One was a man of about five-foot-nine,
bearded, the beard grey-flecked and neatly trimmed, stocky and
neatly dressed, belting a Leech and a Rigdon revolver. The
other man was tall, gangling and with a drooping moustache
which looked as if it might have been trimmed last for celebra-
ting the first battle of Bull Run. He was also neatly dressed
and the walnut-butted Colt 1860 Army revolver in his holster
didn't look as if it took any rust there.

'Howdy,' greeted Waco, as the bearded man moved the pegs over the scoreboard. 'A gent asked me to check these in with you.'

The two old men looked at the revolvers and knives Waco dumped on the desk before them. The bearded man reached out a finger and poked them around, with a grunted explosion of sound.

'Waugh! Looks like they comed off that tolerable fierce gent as was terrorising the town.'

'Waal I swan,' the other went on. 'Tell you he'd go to riling somebody afore he was done, Bix.'

'Yup, that you did, Simon,' replied the bearded man wisely, looking up at Waco. 'Anyhow, ole Simon here,' he waved a hand to his friend, 'allowed we should maybe up and do something.'

'Yup,' agreed Simon. 'But Bix, him being first deputy, said we should do like that limey, Francis Drake, and finish us off our game.'

'Sure, didn't seem no rush at all,' Bix drawled. 'See, we allowed that long afore we could get done here, Mr. Von Schnabel'd be fetching these things in.'

'And does the said Mr. Von Schnabel often do things like that?' asked Waco.

'Oftener 'n' often,' Bix answered, appraising Waco with keen eyes. 'Real brave gent, Mr. Von Schnabel. Four or five times since the sheriff disappeared we had hard gunmen running the town and he come along to disarm them real slick.' He sent a sput of tobacco juice into the spittoon. 'Now me'n ole Simon here, we're just a couple of wored-out deputies, got past it and ready for setting by the stove and hard-wintering.'

'We just ain't up to our work at all,' finished Simon.

'That's your word, or Mr. Von Schnabel's?' asked Waco.

'His,' grunted Simon. 'Don't say it in so many words. Just hints real strong like that the town needs a young man around to handle the law.'

'Same young man being him, I'd reckon.'

'Son, you a sure-enough prophet,' grunted Bix. 'Didn't catch your name.'

'They call me Drifter Smith.'

Grins came to the faces of the two men as they eyed Waco

up and down. Bix shifted his chaw of tobacco around in his mouth, then remarked, 'War over to Kansas a couple or more years back. Saw a bunch of Texas buttons tame down a wild bunch of them fighting pimps the cowtowns have for lawmen. Only one of that bunch warn't called Drifter Smith.'

'Then there's that tough Arizona Ranger who was making a name for hisself and who the Pinkertons,' here Simon spat into the spittoon, 'wants to talk with. Only his name ain't Drifter Smith either.'

'You're both a pair of whiskery ole goats,' laughed Waco. 'You knew who I was all along.'

'Nigh on, nigh on,' Bix answered. 'It could be because we got us a real good memory for faces—or because Miss Ella done sent word we'd likely be meeting up with you real soon.'

'We might be all wored out,' remarked Simon wisely, 'but we ain't dead yet.'

' 'Cepting from the neck up,' growled Waco. 'You know the Pinkertons want me. Do you still need another deputy?'

'Surely we could use a younger man around,' Bix replied soberly. 'The sheriff ain't just tax gathering, he's dead. I found his body in the river four miles down from town. We kept it quiet, let on he was away on business. The elections come off in a fortnight and if he's not back, which same he won't be, Von Schnabel looks like he could get in. The fence-sitters won't have no other choice. If somebody like Drifter Smith was to sit in as Ella Baker's man they'd have to come into line one way or the other.'

'If I sit in I don't do it as anybody's man,' Waco warned. 'I don't play sides when I'm handling a law badge.'

'And she don't want you to,' replied Bix. 'But comes election and after it, if Von Schnabel gets in, them as aren't for him'll be agin him and there won't be much left for them to do but up and get out.'

Simon was looking out of the window, he grinned at the other two and remarked. 'Talk of the devil and Mr. Von Schnabel appears.'

Waco moved, from the desk, walking across the room to study the wanted posters on the wall. Bix Smith swept the weapons from the desk into the top drawer and took up the cards, even as the office door opened.

Studying Von Schnabel from the corner of his eye, Waco saw a tall, broad, stiffly-erect man in the dress of a successful gambler, with close-cropped hair and a scar which added to rather than detracted from his handsome features. The face told a story, spelling martinet army officer, the kind who would command but never lead men. He did not wear a visible weapon.

Halting by the desk he glanced at the cards that lay before the two deputies and snapped, 'There is a gunman terrorising the town. What're you going to do about it?'

'Gunman?' asked Simon mildly.

'What's he look like?' Bix went on.

'A stocky man, a skin hunter and carrying two Colts, and bowie knife and an Arkansas toothpick. He claims he wants to kill a sheriff and he's headed for the Twin Bridge Saloon.'

'With all them weapons he could likely do it,' Bix drawled.

'Could cut lawmen down four at a time,' Simon finished.

Waco listened and grinned. The two deputies certainly gave the impression they were well past their best. He did not move or say anything, for he wanted to know what the German's game was.

Von Schnabel snorted. His voice was hard, commanding and used to ordering, not asking. 'It would appear I must go and do the work of the sheriff's office once again. Then perhaps the people of the town will realise that a sheriff who spends weeks away from town, and two old deputies, are of no use to them. I'll go to the Twin Bridge Saloon and bring the man's weapons back for you.'

'You'd have a walk for nothing,' Bix answered, lifting the two guns and two knives from the desk drawer. 'That young feller just brought them in for us.'

For the first time Von Schnabel looked at Waco, then back down at the weapons which lay on the desk. Waco came forward, halting by Bix's side and said, 'I'd have took his belt but I was scared his pants'd come down and start all the ladies in to blushing.'

Bix chuckled. 'This here's our new deputy.'

'New deputy?' Von Schnabel snorted. 'Who hired him?'

'You know the rules. In the absence of the sheriff, the first deputy can hire extra help if he needs it. And like you say, we need a young man around,' Bix explained. 'And I'm first deputy.'

'Do you know this young man?'

'Sure do, Mr. Von Schnabel. He's one of my kin. One of the Smiths from Smithville, Smith County, Texas. Tolerable large family us Smiths be. This here's Cousin Sefiry Anne's boy, Drifter.'

Von Schnabel felt puzzled. To make an alibi while his men either killed or chased Lynn Baker out of town—leaving the way clear for Wharton's drunk-act and the German's dramatic intervention—Von Schnabel visited another saloon, gave out that he had fired Kyte and joined a poker game. He did not know how his plan went wrong, only that another man appeared to have scooped up the credit.

Before he could say another word he heard the rapid drumming of hooves. A large party of men riding at full gallop came tearing along the street outside. It was clear from the angry yells that the riders were not taking care to avoid the other citizens in their wild and reckless ride through the town.

'What the hell?' Bix growled.

'More trouble, I daresay,' Von Schnabel barked. 'It is a bad thing when the local cowhands care so little for the law that they tear about to the danger of the public. All this wild hoorawing of the town should be brought to an end.'

'Sure,' Waco agreed. 'It's near on as bad as setting up five men to gun down a girl and leave clear the way for a drunk-acting show-off to make trouble.'

Von Schnabel's face was a study of emotions. If Waco had stepped up and hit him in the face with a sock full of bull droppings he could not have been more surprised. Before he could say a word to this statement, which hit right at the plan he'd so carefully laid with his men, there was an interruption. The door of the office was thrown open and a man dashed in.

'Mormons!' he yelled. 'There's a big bunch of them in the square. Allow they're going to fire the Twin Bridge Saloon and kill Miss Ella.'

CHAPTER THREE

DRIFTER SMITH INTERVENES

WACO glanced at the two old deputies, then spoke to Von Schnabel. 'Maybe you'd best go down there and take their guns from them, mister.'

Although Von Schnabel wanted to take up Waco's challenge, he realised the affair might be considerably more risky than disarming his own men as they 'terrorised' the town. Fear did not hold him back, but the thought that the law's attempt might fail acted as a deterrent.

'Bah! Why should I do the work of the sheriff's office?' he snorted. 'There are three of you here and that should be enough. I pay heavy taxes to keep three men in office, why should I have to do their work? What are you going to do about this, Smith?'

'That I haven't decided, yet,' Waco admitted. 'And won't until I get down there and can take a look. Coming, Cousin Bix?'

'Soon as I get me walking cane and spectacles,' replied Bix, going to the wall rack and taking down a ten-gauge shotgun. He broke it, caught the box of shells Simon threw, inserted two into the barrels, put the rest into his pocket and closed the breech. He followed Waco from the office without bothering about the missing walking cane or spectacles.

After the two men left. Von Schnabel let out an angry snort and stalked from the room. Watching the German pass the office window, Simon gave a quiet, contented chuckle.

'Must want to get back to his poker game,' Simon mused, then a grin came to his face. 'That lil ole Drifter Smith surely sat him back on his heels.'

A heated discussion raged in the Twin Bridge Saloon as the crowd related Waco's recent achievements and suggested various exponents of the art of fast draw as his true identity. Taking a chance to extol 'Drifter Smith's' virtues to her friends on the board of County Commissioners, Ella saw no need to interfere with the general discussion until one of the crowd offered Dusty Fog as being Waco's real name. Ella realised she must change the subject before somebody recalled the boy named Waco who once rode with the Rio Hondo gun wizard. So she took the quickest way to peace by calling for drinks on the house with which to toast Drifter Smith. That ended the discussion. Before it could start again, hooves thundered in the square and several horses halted outside the saloon.

'You in there!' a voice bellowed from outside. 'Come out, for we are going to burn down this place of evil.'

'Mormons!' yelled a man, staring through the window.

While the milder spirits in the crowd showed concern, most of the men stated willingness to back Ella in defence of her saloon. Knowing there would be hot-heads in her backing, the woman gave a warning.

'No trouble, boys!' she warned. 'I can straighten this out.'

With Lynn at her side and some fifteen men following, Ella stepped from the saloon and looked at the dozen or more bearded, sombrely dressed, hard-eyed Mormons who sat their horses in line before the building, each man belting a revolver and cradling a Winchester on his arm. A thin old man sat in the centre of the line, his face working in anger.

Although Ella met the old man's accusing glare without visible flinching, she felt very concerned. For deeply religious people the Mormons could handle their end in any man's fight and the weapons they carried were far more than a mere bluffing threat.

'What's your trouble, Elder?' asked Ella.

'Scarlet woman,' replied the Elder, voice pitched high with rage. 'A man of my people lost money in your house of sin.'

Ella nodded. 'Sure, he came in with a big roll and lost it playing poker.'

The angry murmur which rose from the Mormons met grim silence from Ella's party who all knew the woman ran an honest place and that the money was won fairly.

'It was my son!' yelled the Mormon Elder. 'I sent him into

23

town to buy some supplies and instead of doing so he was lured inside your saloon by one of the painted women and stripped of his wealth.'

'That's right, he lost his roll. But he lost it fairly.'

The Elder's face was almost black with rage, his fists, gripping the rifle, shook and Ella thought he would lift it to shoot her down as she stood on the porch. Behind her the men tensed ready to go into action.

'You lie!' the Elder shouted. 'You who batten on the flesh of men. Whose painted women rob the poor fools who are enticed into your den of evil——'

'Shut your mouth, old man!' hissed Lynn. 'Open it any more and you'll be picking lead out of your back teeth.'

Waco and Bix Smith came along the street at a run. The young Texan had taken time out to collect the ·45·75 Winchester Centennial rifle from his saddleboot, for he knew that a rifle was an effective means of stopping a mob, almost as effective as the ten-gauge Bix carried.

On reaching the square, Waco took in the situation and knew what must be done. Tossing his rifle to Bix, Waco vaulted on to the Guesthouse's hitching rail, stepped on to a tethered horse's saddle from which he caught hold of the building's balcony and hauled himself over its rail. Being interested in their own affairs, none of the crowd before the Twin Bridge saw the arrival of the law or noticed Bix toss Waco the rifle, then dart across the street.

Resting his left leg on the balcony rail, Waco sighted the rifle and fired two shots, sending dust spurts leaping on either side of the Mormons.

'Up here!' Waco called, rather unnecessarily. All eyes turned to him, seeing the way he stood, the way the rifle was held. He'd fired two shots, but, even with the new model Winchester there were still ten more bullets in the magazine tube and each bullet was powered by a charge of seventy-five grains of powder. 'Nobody make a move.'

'What do you want, Gentile?' yelled back the Elder.

'Boot the rifles!' Waco answered, and sent a bullet to knock the Winchester from a Mormon's hands as the man started to turn and raise the weapon. 'I'll kill the next man to try anything—and that goes for the saloon porch. You! That red-headed feller at the left!'

Knowing Waco meant what he said, the man in question took his hand from his gun.

None of the Mormons offered to boot their rifles and Waco knew why. To do so would put them at the mercy of the men on the porch.

'Mrs. Baker, ma'am!' Waco called. 'Tell all your friends to go back inside and take a drink.'

'Says who?' one of Ella's party asked, noticing the lack of any badge of authority upon the Texan.

'Says Cousin Drifter!'

Bix Smith peered around the end of the Twin Bridge Saloon, his old ten-gauge held hip high but the bore lined on the men.

Seeing the way Waco wanted to handle the affair, Ella told her friends to go back inside the saloon. They noted the grim determination on both lawmen's faces, knew neither would hesitate to do his duty, and went without question. That left the way clear for dealing with the Mormons.

The men clearly did not take to this idea at all. They none of them trusted the Mormons, but Ella seemed sure of herself. So all but Brentford trooped towards the door. He paused and looked up at Waco, then asked, 'Reckon he'd shoot me if I don't go, Ella?'

'About them rifles, Elder!' called Waco, a hard note creeping into his voice. 'I'm getting quite sick of asking.'

Before the Elder could speak, a buggy driven by a big, burly Mormon came tearing around the corner. The other Mormons drew back, showing considerable respect to this man as he brought his buggy to a halt between them and the saloon. There was a grim look in his eyes as he studied the men and his voice was hard, commanding, as he asked:

'Eli, what does all this mean?'

The rifles slid into saddleboots at the arrival of the man in the buggy. Waco saw his chance to move in, so called, 'Hold 'em down, Cousin Bix.'

'Surely so, Cousin Drifter,' Bix yelled back, grinning, for he knew who the man in the buggy was. 'Come ahead.'

Slipping the safety catch on his rifle, Waco walked along the balcony until clear of the horses then dropped to the ground.

He crossed the square and halted by the buggy, but looked at the thin elder.

'What's all this about?' he asked.

'That's their bishop, Cousin Drifter,' remarked Bix, indicating the man in the buggy, as he joined the others on the porch.

'That doesn't answer the question,' replied Waco. 'What's it about, Elder?'

'One of our people was cheated by this Gentile bitch——'

Lynn began an angry objection but Waco stopped her before she could speak. He looked at the old man, his eyes cold and warning, his voice hard as he drawled:

'That's a hard name, Elder, and a serious charge. Whereat's this man who says he was cheated?'

The Elder looked uncomfortable. 'It was my son. He's not here.'

'Why not?' asked Waco. 'Appears to me that a man growed enough to take hard likker and play poker's old enough to come and talk for hisself.'

'He was my son. I sent him into town to buy supplies,' replied the Elder, but his voice was not so hard now. 'Instead he was enticed into this den of sin——'

Lynn's gun came from her holster. 'You say that again,' she hissed, 'and I'm going to let air into you.'

'Leather it!' Waco snapped and, much to Ella's surprise, Lynn obeyed. 'Allus been told it takes a man who's sinned to know it, gal.'

'Eli,' the Bishop spoke up. 'Your son is a man grown. He should be trusted to come into town and buy supplies without losing the money.'

'Tell us about your son, Elder,' suggested Ella. 'He came to town and lost money in my saloon, you say.'

'Five hundred dollars,' snarled the Elder. 'Taken by a painted hussy——'

'Mister!' Waco snapped, his voice hard now. 'You tell what you've got to tell and stop name calling. I'm not going to ask again.'

'I want to hear about the money your son lost, Eli,' said the Bishop.

'I'll tell you all about it,' growled Bix Smith, moving forward. 'Your son's a tall, black-haired young jasper with a cast in his left eye, ain't he?' The Mormon nodded. 'Sure, he came in yesterday, got him his likker along the street and come out with a man who was taking him to Dillis' place to gamble. I knowed that he'd lose his eyeballs down there and took him along to the Twin Bridge. Miss Ella always gives a square deal. Your son couldn't play poker with a damn; he even tried to cheat Ella and she cleaned him out in three deals.'

There was an angry rumble from the Mormons at this, for it appeared that one of their kind had been swindled out of money. The Bishop frowned, his eyes going to Ella, then to Waco, as he opened his mouth to speak.

'Now hold on a doggone minute,' Bix ordered. 'Let a man finish afore you starts jumping to conclusions. Ella put the money, less ten per cent for her trouble in an envelope and brought it to the jail. We got it locked in the safe right now, just waiting for you to come and collect it.'

'Sounds tolerable fair for a crooked gambling house, don't it?' asked Waco.

'More than fair,' replied the Bishop, then looked at the Elder. 'I will want a full accounting of why these men were brought here in such a manner.'

'Old man,' put in Waco, looking hard at the Elder. 'You see how near you come to getting bad trouble? You got one of your men's rifles bust for him. It could have got worse than that. You could have stirred up bad trouble between your folks and us here in town. Trouble that could have spread through Utah and every other place where there's Mormons.'

'Words of wisdom from a Gentile,' said the Bishop gently. 'I agree with every word of it. You will pay for a new rifle for the man. I will collect your money from the jail and bring it to you. Now leave and take the others with you.'

Knowing better than to argue with a Bishop, the old man turned and rode away, followed by his men. The watching crowd once more began to talk about the blond Texan they knew as Drifter Smith.

'Now, Bishop,' Ella said. 'I'll come to the jail with you and see the money handed over.'

'If you climb in, ma'am,' he replied, 'I'll drive you.'

Simon looked up with interest as Waco's party, swollen by

the presence of Ella and the Bishop, entered the office.

'What happened?' he asked. 'I heard a shot.'

'I've heard one myself, so don't get all puffed up and boastful about it,' Waco replied and ignored Simon's grunt as he took the envelope Bix collected from the safe. 'Count the money, sir, and sign the receipt, please.'

The Bishop took the envelope and signed the receipt, then turned to Waco and smiled. 'You are a brave man. You risked the wrath of your people as well as mine in stopping trouble.'

'That's what I get paid for,' Waco replied. 'The law's the same for everybody.'

'Perhaps. But there are many lawmen who would not agree with you. The Elder is a foolish man and should never have brought the men to town in such a manner. It is people like him who help breed hatred between our church and your people. I would rather it had not happened.'

'No harm was done, 'cept to that feller's rifle,' replied Waco. 'But the next time your people come to town with a complaint, tell them to bring it to the sheriff's office and we'll tend to it. I'm not having wild riding and trouble caused in my town.'

'I will remember, so will my people,' the Bishop promised, looking at Waco with respect. The young Gentile sounded so sure of himself, so certain of his ability to handle any trouble, yet he did not wear any badge of office. 'I will go back to my people now. I think Two Forks will be a better place when this is over and with a man like you running the law.'

After the Mormon Bishop left, Waco turned to Ella and grinned. 'I've not got me a badge yet.'

'Bix can tend to that,' she replied. 'You handled that well. I wonder if the Mormons are losing stock?'

'Are the others?'

'Sure, most of the local ranchers have told me they've been losing some. Not much but a little,' answered Ella. 'You'll be expected to do something about that when you take office.'

'If I do,' corrected Waco. 'I reckon the folks are blaming the Mormons?'

'For everything, from losing stock to the bad weather.'

Waco looked at the woman, realising that she was probably the best-informed person in the County. There were things he wanted to know about this business, small details that he wanted clearing up and this appeared to be a good time to get them cleared.

'If Von Schnabel's so well backed, how come he doesn't just take over as the sheriff, the old one being dead?'

'Because only four people know he is dead,' replied Ella, sitting at the desk. 'Bix, Simon, me—and the man who killed him.'

'We're a big county. It would take a man quite a long time to make a full tour of it,' Ella explained, smiling at Waco's caution. 'Besides, there've been at least three letters from him, explaining his absence.'

'I may be dumb,' Waco said slowly. 'But how did you come to get letters from the sheriff after he was killed?'

'There's a man in town—and I won't tell you who—— He made his living signing other people's cheques. He's a friend of mine and made up letters from the sheriff which passed even Von Schnabel's rigid inspection. So the killing was no use. The killer could hardly come out and say, "Those letters are forgeries, because I killed the sheriff." So Von Schnabel had to hold back, could not do anything until the re-election took place.'

Waco smiled. Ella Baker was a shrewd woman who appeared to have covered all the bets in the game. With her able backing there was a chance that he might be able to pull the sheriff's chore out of the bag. This looked like a nice section for a man to settle in and it would be lively enough even for Waco's reckless tastes.

'You know what was planned for this morning?' she asked after a moment.

'Sure,' answered Waco and his voice was suddenly hard. 'Those five were in there to force a fight with your girl or scare her clean out of town. And I reckon they'd have had to fight her, she wouldn't scare. Then that loud-sounding *hombre* was to come in and start to shoot your place up. You'd have your hands full one way or the other and couldn't handle him. Then Von Schnabel'd show, disarm him and run him out of town. The folks'd say that Von Schnabel was some man, he doesn't like you but still goes and helps you out.'

'You've called the play just right,' Ella said seriously. 'Now you can see that you're up against a desperate and dangerous man.'

'Yes'm,' agreed Waco. 'And I aim to beat him. I wouldn't want to lose to a man who'd set a girl up to be killed.'

CHAPTER FOUR

COMING INTO THE PUBLIC EYE

ON the morning after his arrival in Two Forks, Waco lay in a bed in the deputies' quarters of the jail and looked to where the coffee pot steamed upon the stove, lit by Simon who had been on night watch.

'Hey, third deputy,' growled a voice from the corner of the room. 'You awake yet?'

'Nope,' replied Waco, turning his head to eye Bix grimly.

'Well, when you are, how about getting up and making the coffee?' growled Bix, peering over the blankets with a belligerent glare.

'Don't you forget I won't be third deputy for long,' warned Waco. 'Then I'll see there's some changes made.'

Bix grinned. 'Waal, until you are sheriff, I'm still first deputy, so you jest up and make the coffee. Should do it when you gets to be sheriff. Show some respect for your elders.'

'Respect?' Waco grunted, rolling from the bed and reaching for his levis. 'Respect for a worn out ole goat like you?'

The young man pulled on his pants, socks and boots. He stretched, the hard, powerful muscles of his young frame rippling under his skin. He looked at the coffee-pot, saw it was not quite ready, so asked, 'Where'd a man get a wash and shave?'

'Pump out thar,' replied Bix disgustedly. 'Don't hold with all this here washing. Allus allow it'd weaken a man.'

Ignoring Bix's warning, Waco went out back where, after caring for his paint, he washed and shaved. On his return, he had just started to make the coffee when he heard a voice from the office.

'Hey! You in there!'

Recognising the voice, Waco thrust one of his Colts into his waistband. Then he entered the office and brought a hurried change in Ben Wharton's attitude. Wharton might have chanced taking an arrogant line with the old deputies, but knew the same would be doomed to certain failure if tried against the blond Texan.

'Come along to pay for the damage and collect me guns.'

'Sure,' Waco drawled, eyeing Wharton with disdain. 'Figger thirty dollars'd cover the damage you did, the fine you'd get from the Judge and all. Shell out and look happy.'

'Thirty dollars!' Wharton yelped. 'That'll not leave me with but coffee money, Drifter.'

'I'm sorry for you, real sorry,' Waco replied in a voice which showed anything but sorrow. 'Pay up and drink water. You all staying on in town?'

'Waal——!' Wharton began, pulling money out to pay and watching Waco dump his two guns and the knives on the desk top. 'I ain't sure what I'll be doing.'

'All right. Take your guns,' Waco drawled, then gave a grim warning. 'But remember this well. Sober, drunk or *playing drunk*, don't never try and run no blazer on my town again. The next time I'll jail you—if you try it three times, I'll kill you.'

'Sure,' he growled, not liking the way two of the words were emphasised. 'We all makes mistakes, Drifter.'

'Yep,' agreed Waco, seeing Simon coming along the street by the windows. 'I don't hold it again your mammy and pappy though, they didn't know.'

Scowling, Wharton paid his fine, scooped up his weapons and left the office. By the time Waco returned to the deputies' quarters at the rear of the building, he found that the swamper from the Twin Bridge Saloon had brought breakfast and his fellow workers sat at the table. None spoke until they had finished eating.

'Some comings and goings back of the Guesthouse last night,' Simon remarked.

Waco pushed aside his plate and started to roll a cigarette. He looked at Bix, ignoring Simon and asked, 'Is that supposed to interest us?'

'Hell, you pair ain't got the sense to know nothing,' Simon growled disgustedly. 'It's the night-hawk as does all the work.'

'He wants to tell us something,' said Waco mockingly to Bix. 'Do we act all polite and listen to him or do we say nothing and hope he'll go away?'

'Won't get no peace until we listen,' answered Bix in a tone of resignation.

They both sat back with a well-done look of interest on their faces, but Simon took out his old pipe and began to clean it carefully, paying great attention to the condition of the bowl. He extracted a block of thick, black-looking tobacco and a knife, carefully carving a pipe full and grinding it with exaggerated care, tamped it home, lit the pipe and sat back.

'Anyways,' he said, 'you wouldn't be interested in what I got to say.'

'Likely won't,' agreed Waco, 'but we aren't going to get any peace until we've heard it.'

Simon sniffed in disgust. Then decided he'd condescend to tell his great secret to the other two.

'War a wagon out back of the Guesthouse last night.'

'Again?' grunted Bix wisely.

'It happened afore?' asked Waco.

'Naw,' snorted Bix. 'I jest said it 'cause I'm young and likes to hear me voice talking.'

'Been three that I knows of,' Simon went on, studying Waco in disgust. 'I saw them. Might have been others. Don't know what's in them.'

'Could be gambling gear,' suggested Waco.

'Why deliver it at night, if that was all it was?' Simon grunted.

'Know one bunch who always deliver at night, or did. Cap'n Bert 'n' Billy Speed caught up with them. It was a crooked gambling syndicate, only now they don't work at anything except making hair bridles.'

By which the two old deputies knew that the members of the syndicate, after falling foul of Captain Bertram Mosehan, were now in jail and engaged in the task of making hair bridles for the benefit of the Territory of Arizona.

'Might be what Von Schnabel's doing,' Bix remarked. 'Although I never saw anything crooked about any of his games—and I knows a might about crooked gambling, boy.'

'Twarn't gambling gear anyways,' Simon answered, coming

33

to his feet and walking towards the door. 'Leastways,' he went on, opening the door and picking something up, carrying it back and dumping it on the table. 'I don't know what game he'd be playing with this.'

If Simon hoped to surprise his friends, he succeeded. Waco's cigarette fell unheeded from his fingers and Bix ignored the hot coffee he spilled down his shirt front. The drum-like metal object Simon dumped before them did not form part of a piece of gambling equipment—unless it be some game involving the use of a Gatling gun's Accles positive-feed magazine.

'What the hell would Von Schnabel want with a Gatling gun?' Waco asked.

'Mebbee aims to be the best-armed sheriff in the West,' suggested Bix.

'Could aim to outhunt Buffler Bill, straight killing run,' went on Simon.

'And you pair could be a whisky set of goats without the sense of a seam squirrel,' growled Waco. 'I didn't know there were any Gatling guns for sale.'

'Looks like there is,' Bix drawled dryly. 'The Army's got some.'

'Sure, but a man couldn't walk into a hardware store and order a couple over the counter. Sides which, they run to around a thousand dollar a-piece,' Waco said. 'Wonder why Von Schnabel bought one. Is that wagon still there?'

'Nope. They started to check it over, then it pulled out over the cattle bridge to the other end of town.'

Waco looked thoughtful. He was worried by the arrival of the wagon, and not able to make up his mind what the reason was behind it. There was one thing he could do; get his horse and head to the cattle bridges, so called because they were at the other end of the town from the river junction and allowed trail herds to be moved over the rivers without having to make a swim, or go through the town. Out beyond the town he might possibly be able to find the tracks and follow the wagon to its destination. The mystery of the Gatling gun must be solved, he was sure of that.

'What's Von Schnabel do, does he own anything besides the saloon?' he asked.

'Got him a spread up in the back country, small place,' Bix

replied. 'Got a bunch of hard-cases works at it. Most of them are Germans like him. I was only out that way once. He mostly pays off his taxes, pays higher than I'd thought he'd need with a place like that. Saved the sheriff going out to make tax assessment. I ain't been up that way for over a year.'

'Ain't it time you pair went to work?' Simon asked bitingly. 'Let the old night-hawk get his sleep. It's him that does all the work.'

Waco pushed back his chair and went to strap on his gunbelt, then he took his hat and left the room. Bix went to the office to tidy up and fill in the office log. For once there was something to put in, for Drifter Smith had had a busy time the previous day.

The Guesthouse was as big, clean-looking and well arranged as the Twin Bridge Saloon, which it faced. Its bar was empty and deserted of all but a few members of the staff who were at the tables, getting prepared for the arrival of the day's trade.

Von Schnabel sat at his usual table by the side of the room, arranged so that he could get a clear view of both the doors and the windows which faced the Twin Bridge Saloon. Matt Kyte was seated facing his boss, a worried look on his face as he tried to explain away his failure of the previous day. A pretty, red-haired dance-hall girl was seated at the next table to them, reading a gaudy-covered blood-and-thunder book. The two men ignored her for they were speaking in German, and, to the best of their knowledge, the girl, Kitty Regan, could speak only English with a strong accent of the Ould Sod.

'I could do nothing,' Kyte stated, trying to think of a way to show his actions in a good light. 'The Texan is fast with his guns. Then there was the girl, she was ready to help him and the three women behind the bar.'

It was at that moment Von Schnabel saw Waco pass in front of the windows. The frown on his face deepened and he answered. 'That man is an inconvenience. He twice stopped a plan I made.'

'It would be best if he died.'

'It would have been best had he died yesterday,' barked Von Schnabel. 'Why is he still alive? There were five of you.'

'He is faster than any man I ever saw. And he took us by surprise.'

'Is there not one man among our people who will kill him?' asked Von Schnabel. 'The new man, Wharton, he is said to be fast with his gun.'

'He won't risk it, not without more men to help him,' Kyte replied. 'I asked him to try an ambush but he wants more men before he dare try.'

'The fool!' snapped the saloon keeper. 'And have it said that my men killed the only man who might oppose me in the election. These ignorant peasants are not such big fools. There are even some of them who do not believe I discharged you and the others yesterday. And this Drifter Smith, he suspects that you and Wharton were connected.'

Kyte thought his boss under-estimated the intelligence of the people of the West, but did not say so. Von Schnabel regarded them as being stupid, ignorant, incapable of thinking for themselves. That was why Kyte did not like the idea of the previous day's plan. Not because he might have to shoot and kill a girl, but because he doubted if anyone would believe he really had been fired by Von Schnabel.

'That damned Texan's smart,' he said.

Von Schnabel nodded. 'Smart and intelligent,' he agreed and sounded surprised. The young Texan was far from being a stupid, dull-witted peasant of the kind Von Schnabel was used to dealing with in Germany. 'But who is he? I've never heard of a man called Drifter Smith and such a one would become known.'

'He might be a wanted outlaw,' answered Kyte. 'I don't know if he is and I don't know how we could find out.'

'Would the people vote for him?'

'They might. He's a Westerner and the sort of man they can understand. They do not understand you.'

'That is true,' grunted Von Schnabel. 'He must be killed.'

'In here?' Kyte asked doubtfully.

'At Dillis' place,' Von Schnabel replied and explained his plan.

Neither man noticed the girl leave the next table and go through the rear door of the room, being more engrossed in their plans for removing Waco.

Temporarily putting aside thoughts of the Gatling gun, Waco made his rounds of the town. Wherever he went, whispers followed in his wake:

'That's Drifter Smith. The Texas man who broke up Kyte's bunch when they went to try and wreck the Twin Bridge Saloon, then backed down a——'

And so the recounting of Drifter Smith's exploits went on. At noon Waco entered the Twin Bridge, glanced at the gun-checking sign and threw a wink in Lynn's direction, bringing a poked-out tongue in reply. Ella came to Waco's table as a waitress took his order for lunch.

'Did I ever tell you I worked in a tent show back east when I was a girl?' she asked. 'Ran what they call a mitt camp. Used to tell fortunes, palms, stars, tea-leaves—or cards.'

'Never believed much about that stuff, ma'am,' Waco replied, wondering what was coming, for Ella was doing more than just making idle chatter.

'You'd be surprised how it works sometimes,' Ella answered, splitting the deck and giving it a feather-fingered gambler's riffle that was a joy to behold. More so to a man who knew crooked gambling moves as well as Waco did. The riffle looked quite natural, the cards falling together, but when the time came to block them up into a single pile Ella brought off as neat a 'pull-through' as Waco was ever privileged to see. Her hands moved fast, slipping the two blocks through each other and replacing them so that the cards were in the same order as when she started the riffle.

'I see danger in your life,' she said, dealing the cards face up. 'I see years of adventure behind you and more to come.' She laid out the cards, using the terms of the fortune teller to cover what she knew of Waco's past life. Then she turned up the ace and king of spades. 'I see death. Death and a small dark man,' she went on, her voice changing slightly. 'The cards give a warning to you, Drifter Smith. Beware of a small dark man. Beware when he scratches the back of his left hand.'

With that, Ella scooped the cards together and riffled them once more, looking directly at Waco all the time. She knew he was taking more than just a friendly interest in her words, reading the warning she was giving him.

'What're you getting at, ma'am?' he asked.

'Just what the cards say,' Ella answered, sounding as if the subject was closed. 'How'd you like the town?'

37

Ella made no further mention of her warning and nothing happened all afternoon. Two shots brought Waco on the run as he made his evening rounds. The affected saloon was Dillis' Blackjack, by repute the toughest, most crooked in town. Looking through a window, Waco saw the customers crowded back against the walls, with the exception of a small, scared-looking townsman who sat at a table in the centre of the room. The man stared at the line of glasses on the table, one of which had been shattered by a bullet from the gun of the young hard-case who'd backed Kyte at the Twin Bridge.

'When I've bust them, I'll shoot one off the top of your head,' the youngster told his victim and lined his gun once more.

Stepping quietly through the doors, Waco intended to move in behind the young man and buffalo him; but had the chance spoiled by a slick-haired jasper wearing a loud check town suit and who yelled:

'He's drunk, deputy. Get him out of here!'

Waco could have cursed. His entry had been unnoticed by the young gunman and without that shout he might have got up close enough to end the trouble with a well-placed Colt barrel over the head. Now the youngster was turning, his hand hefting the gun to line on Waco, a sneer coming to his face.

'Yeah, deputy,' he said, his speech slurred and whisky-dulled. 'You get me out of here—if you can.'

Slowly Waco moved towards the young man, eyes never leaving his face, every sense alert for the first sign which would warn him to get clear. The young gunman backed off, his gun still lined but the hammer was not drawn back. Waco followed him up, driving him back step by step until they were both past the table. Then Waco halted, sitting on the table, hands behind him, resting on the edge.

'Who put you up to all this foolishness, boy?' he asked. 'Was it Kyte?'

'Up to what?' asked the young gunman.

'Fooling like this. You don't want to shoot this gent here. You're supposed to be gunning me down, aren't you?'

'Get him out of here, deputy!' Dillis, the owner, shouted.

Once more Waco could have cursed at the man. The sudden shout made the young gunman start and fumble at the hammer of the Colt. It was then Waco saw what was happening; Dillis was in on this play.

'Get your men to help me, or leave me do it my way,' he answered.

'I want him out of it,' Dillis answered, sticking his hands into the pockets of his loud checked suit. 'Come on, get to it.'

'Why sure,' said Waco, then looked behind the young gunman. 'Don't cut him down, Bix!'

Starting to turn, the youngster realised his mistake; but the whisky, drunk to prime him for facing Waco, slowed his reactions. Waco rolled backwards from the table and heaved it over at the hard-case. Yelping, the youngster fended it off. Following up the table, Waco drew his right Colt and laid its barrel effectively across the other's jaw. A low murmur of approval rose from the crowd as the hard-case dropped. Ignoring public approval, Waco snapped :

'All right, this place is closed. Clear it.'

'What do you mean, closed!' Dillis snarled, moving forward.

'You heard me. I'm counting to five and I want this place empty by the time I get to three.'

A short, dark man in gambler's dress ranged himself alongside Dillis. 'You want a helluva lot for a john law.'

'Who're you?' Waco answered.

'This's my partner, Keg Bullock,' Dillis introduced, a sneer on his lips. 'You'd have to take up closing me out with him.'

Waco studied the small man, the small, *dark* man. 'That so?' he asked. 'We'd best have you closed down then.'

Slowly Keg Bullock lowered his right hand to scratch the back of his left. It was an apparently harmless gesture which might have gone unnoticed but Waco remembered what Ella Baker had said, remembered the message of the cards.

Keg Bullock's hand went into his sleeve cuff and the Remington Double Derringer slid into his palm. It was a fast, well-done move, and at that range, even so low powered a weapon as the stubby Derringer was not likely to miss.

Waco's hands made a flickering blur of movement. The bar lights glinted dully on the blued barrels of his matched Colts. Flame tore from the barrels of the guns as they came clear and lined, held hip high. Bullock took lead. The force of the bullets picked him up and hurled his body backwards into the bar.

Smoke curled from the barrels of Waco's guns. The gambler slid to the floor, his weapon dropping from his hand. There was not a sound through the saloon. It was all over and done with in less than a second. Keg Bullock, a fast man who had taken the decision in three such affairs, lay dead on the floor, beaten by the tall young Texas man.

The guns whirled back into Waco's holsters. Then he stepped forward, the back of his hand lashed up into Dillis' face, rocking the man into the bar. Waco followed the man up, giving him no chance to make either defence or attack. His right ripped into Dillis' stomach, then whipped up with a punch that snapped the man's head back and hung him half-dazed on the bar.

Bunching his hands on the front of Dillis' coat Waco shook him, then gave a heave which crashed him into the bar once more. The Texan did not raise his voice but every man in the room heard him, so silent were they.

'*Hombre*, your place's closed and it'll stay closed. No man's going to set me up for a kill and get away with it. You'll be out of town by noon tomorrow. If you're not, I'll be looking for you—and I'll spit in your face, every time I see you!'

Dillis made no attempt to defend himself or say a word to Waco. He hung on the bar, blood trickling down his chin and a scared glint in his eyes. His business in Two Forks was very good and he'd be lucky to get any sort of a price for his place in the short time at his disposal. One thing he knew for sure, he was going to be long gone by the time the deadline passed; a Texan did not give out with that particular warning without he meant every single word of it.

Turning, Waco faced the crowd. 'I want this place cleared,' he warned. 'Two of you tote this *hombre* to the jail for me.'

There was a mass departure from the saloon; a man did not argue with a tough peace-officer like Drifter Smith. So they left and Dillis' saloon was closed down permanently; the toughest, most crooked place in the town, yet it was emptied and deserted within fifteen minutes of Waco's arrival. Only a dead body lying in a pool of blood showing that the law was in Two Forks and aimed to stay there.

Von Schnabel heard the news and flew into a rage. Dillis meant nothing to him and knew nothing of his plans, but the man had been a useful ally. Now Dillis was making plans for a rapid departure from the town and wanting a price for his saloon in the threat of telling Drifter Smith who laid on the plan.

Instead of being dead, Drifter Smith was very much alive. Worse, he was even more popular among the many people who wanted to see their town tamed and cleaned up. He was coming into the public eye more and more all the time and Von Schnabel knew that he'd helped make it possible.

CHAPTER FIVE

A BUSY DAY FOR DRIFTER SMITH

In the days which followed, Waco found himself too busy to try to solve the mystery of the Gatling gun's magazine. Posters stating 'DRIFTER SMITH FOR SHERIFF' appeared around town and although Waco had been sponsored by the banker and gunsmith, everybody knew Ella Baker stood behind him. He ran the law fairly and without fear. Folks talked of how he stood against the Ladies Social and Civic Improvement Society when they demanded that he closed the two brothels, stating that as long as the houses comported themselves quietly and honestly he would not interfere with their performance of a needed service. His stand raised him even in the eyes of several husbands sent to lodge formal complaints about his discourtesy. One tricky moment came when an old friend, professional gambler Frank Derringer, shot a man during a card game. Derringer had been in the right and their friendship did not come to light. Although several days in town, Derringer made no mention of Waco's true identity and gave no hint of knowing the Texan.

By the eve of election day Waco knew himself to have built up a strong following in the county. He also found himself thinking that it never rained but what it poured. Not only had all the local ranchers paid off their crews, the cowhands flocking into town for the celebrations, but two freight outfits and a wagon train added their quota to the work on the lawmen's hands.

Early in the evening all three deputies converged on Bonnie Hendrick's brothel, brought by the noise of ten or so cowhands mixed in a fight.

There was no hesitation in the way Waco acted. He was at

the scene ahead of Bix and saw Simon approaching from the other side even as he went into action. He grabbed two of the fighters by the scruffs of their necks, cracked their heads together and pitched them apart. Then he was into the rest, hard fists shooting out and sending the men staggering. His sudden arrival and fast tactics took the fighters completely by surprise. One of them caught a punch and landed flat on his back, his opponent started to throw a punch at Waco, only to get it blocked, then a rock hard fist caught him under his jaw and stretched him flat by the man he'd been fighting.

The fight broke up and the cowhands stood or sat staring at the three lawmen who surrounded them. Every one of the fighting group expected to be hauled off to jail and it came as a surprise when Waco asked:

'What happened?'

'Shucks, twarn't nothing,' one of the hands answered, holding his jaw. 'Me'n the rest of the Lazy J boys here was just coming to Bonnie's and we saw the Box O's here coming. Started in to discussing them out of it. What'd you hit me with, Drifter? I feel like I been kicked by a knobhead.'

Waco could see that there was nothing more serious than friendly rivalry between the two outfits. The fact that fists and not guns were used in the fight showed that only cowhand high-spirits were involved. He'd been on a spree and in such friendly fights himself and knew how little it meant. However, he needed to give them a warning.

'Just get one thing into your fool heads,' he snapped. 'There's a bunch in this town that wants the houses closing down. You bunch pulling fool games like this outside don't help to keep them open.'

Bonnie Hendricks licked her lips and her face flushed angrily. She knew of the moves to get her closed down and had seen other places closed by a man seeking public acclaim during an election. She quite expected that she would either be closed or that a large bribe, termed 'campaign funds', would be called for, even though the Texan had not demanded such so far. He must have been waiting for just such a moment and the bite, when it came, would be very heavy.

'Smith,' she said, meaning to get down to business and to hell with doing it in private, 'I——'

'Howdy, ma'am,' replied Waco, removing his hat. 'Take the boys in and give them something for their heads.'

'You mean you're not closing me down?' she gasped.

'Why for, ma'am?' replied Waco, putting his hat on again. 'They weren't in your place when the fighting started and you'd no part in starting it.'

Bonnie gulped. She was not used to this sort of treatment from a peace-officer, especially as she was known to favour Von Schnabel in the elections. She looked at the cowhands who were getting to their feet, grinning sheepishly at her and at each other.

'Go on in, boys,' she said. 'Tell Jack the drinks are on me.'

Before Bonnie could follow the cowhands into the house Waco stopped her. He gave her a gentle spoken warning. 'One thing, ma'am. You don't have any trouble as long as there's no wild parties, drunk rolling or cat-fights——'

'Did Ella Baker tell you that I allowed those sort of things?'

'Don't recollect Mrs. Baker ever saying anything much about you, except that you and Miss Meg run clean houses,' replied Waco, tipping his hat to her. He took out some money and passed it to the woman. 'Buy the boys a drink on me. Then tell them there's a nice, big, wide open country outside the town limits all set for them to start fighting in.'

A man wearing a striped apron came running up yelling, 'There's going to be some trouble at the Brown Doll Saloon.'

Waco and his deputies turned and headed back towards Colorado Street and the woman watched them go. She'd never come across a lawman like Drifter Smith. Any other, almost every other she'd known, would have closed her; extracted a bribe for allowing her to stay open; or at worst expected her to buy drinks in his name all night. Drifter Smith had done none of these things. He even paid for the round of drinks himself.

The leaders of the two ranch crews were standing at the door of the house. 'Sorry about that, Bonnie,' one said. 'Man, that Drifter Smith sure packs him a mean right hand. There's a whole lot of lawmen who'd have taken us all to jail, some of us with broken heads.'

'Sure would,' agreed the other. 'I tell you, Pete, Drifter Smith's the best man for the Box O.'

Bonnie Hendricks followed the two cowhands into her place

and closed the door, wondering if perhaps Drifter Smith was not the man for her also.

Waco and the other two deputies arrived at the Brown Doll Saloon, one of the larger and better-class places of the town. They forced their way in through the doors in time to prevent a full-scale battle between the cowhands and the saloon staff.

'Hold it!' Waco ordered, coming through the batwings with Bix and Simon fanned out behind him.

Brown, the owner, looked considerably relieved. 'Arrest this bunch, deputy!' he yelled.

'Why?'

'Why?' Brown squealed like a stuck pig. He was not a Von Schnabel supporter and thought merely demanding the arrest of the cowhands would be all Waco needed to hear. 'Why?' he repeated.

'Sure, but that's not the answer.'

'Lookee here, deputy,' said a grizzled old cowhand, stepping forward. 'The bardog got ole Nimble here,' he indicated a vacant-looking cowhand, 'to take a bet for his month's pay on a go of One Flop. Then tried to use a slick cup on him. Ole Nimble surely annoyed the bardog when he starts to whirl that slick cup round and drop out five little old sixes.'

Waco went to the bar, taking the leather dice cup and five dice from the top of the counter. The inside of the cup was smoothed down to a fine finish and Waco knew why. The five dice were loaded to throw sixes when the cup was worked in a special way. The ordinary player would place the dice in the cup, shake them and then throw, counting whatever his score was. At One Flop, just one throw decided the game, the score was added up and the other man must try to beat it. The crooked player counted his opponent's score, then took the cup and instead of shaking, moved it up and down with a rotating action. The centrifugal force lined up the dice with the unweighted six sides ready to throw, then they were thrown out parallel to the bar top, the crook giving a slight forward shove and quick pull back to drop the five sixes in plain view. Usually the cheater would not have the dice all weighted to come out sixes, but must have thought the vacant-looking cowhand would be dumb enough to fall for it.

Waco could imagine the consternation when the lamb for

45

the slaughter used the same method to throw an unbeatable score. It must have been just the same as if a lamb had turned round and pole-axed the butcher.

Waco grinned, slipping the dice in the cup and turning it until he felt the five dice laying dead, then slid them forward. The five sixes were exposed to view and he turned back to Brown. The man was livid with anger.

'That damned cowhand tried to rook me,' he snarled. 'I want him arrested.'

'Sure,' agreed Waco. 'Bix, take the cowhand to jail. Simon, take Mr. Brown along for running a crooked game. The cup's your'n, isn't it?'

Brown looked almost fit to be tied. 'Sure the cup's mine. But I didn't know it was worked on. I'd never even heard of slick cups.'

'Waal, give back the stake money, call off the arrest and thank this cowhand for saving you some bad trouble later on,' Waco drawled. 'It's one or the other.'

The saloon keeper was in an awkward spot. He'd guessed his bartender was swindling customers but was not sure how. The man was very good at his other work and Brown had not wanted to fire him. Now he was left with the choice of letting the charge against Nimble drop, or being jailed himself.

'All right, damn it,' he snarled. 'Forget it. Get them cowhands out of here. I was going to give you my vote tomorrow.'

'Now you don't aim to,' Waco replied.

For all that he was not worried. He might have lost one man's vote but he'd be willing to bet he'd made many more.

The saloon was cleared of hostile cowhands, business was resumed and Brown got rid of his dice cups.

After leaving the Brown Doll, Waco went to the deputies' quarters at the jail and took time out to change his shirt. A slight sound brought Waco's attention to the door, moving with near silent feet in a manner which was not calculated to make Waco feel easy in his mind. People rarely sneaked around the rear of the jail without having some sinister reason for so doing. So Waco took precautions. He moved to the side of the door, flattened against the wall with his right-hand Colt ready for use. His hand reached down towards the door handle, ready to tear it open and go out fast, when he saw something white being slipped under the door: 'DRIFTER SMITH.'

The young Texan did not bend down immediately; he heard the sound of fast departing feet and looked around. His rifle was in its saddleboot and hung above the bed, so he reached out, drawing the Winchester and then used it to pull the letter towards him. He knew that an attempt on his life might be in the offing, a man waiting outside with a gun lined ready to pump lead through the door towards whoever picked up the letter.

There was no shot, nothing at all, as Waco bent and took up the letter. He shoved the rifle back into the boot and sat down on the bed to rip the envelope and take out a plain, cheap sheet of writing paper on which was printed a message in the same neat hand.

'Tomorrow morning the stage will be held up at that drywash three miles out of town. Expect five men in the gang.'

There was no signature and Waco did not expect one. He sniffed at the letter, a smile coming to his lips. The writer took care that the handwriting would not be recognised, but that faint smell of perfume told him all he needed to know.

At that moment, Waco heard voices in the office so stepped through the door to find Bix Smith taking a couple of men to the cells.

'Found 'em rolling a drunk,' the old deputy remarked as he brought the keys of the cells back and laid them on the desk. 'What you got there?'

'A letter from a lady,' Waco replied. 'And it wasn't Mrs. Trenard apologising and telling me all's forgiven. What do you make of this?'

Bix took the letter, reading it, then handed it back and replied wisely, 'The stage's going to be held up tomorrow morning.'

'Naw!' replied Waco, showing his amazement at such brilliance. 'How'd you work that out all on your tired ole self? What do you know about it, Bix?'

'Know the drywash they mean,' the old-timer answered. 'Thought plenty of times how good a place it'd be for a hold-up, 'cepting it's a mite too near town.'

'Reckon I'll go out there in the morning,' Waco remarked. 'Folks might start believing there was no respect for the law happen a bunch of owlhoots pulled a raid so close to town.'

CHAPTER SIX

THE HOLD-UP

Waco got little sleep the night before Election Day, but he'd missed sleep before and doubted if another night would harm him. The jail cells held a fair crowd, mostly drunks who'd been brought in. Some were hauled in asleep; some came quietly, or noisily; just a couple made it the hard way and would have painful heads beyond a mere hangover when they woke, for the three lawmen were busy and applied the barrel of a revolver when it was called for rather than waste time. There was no serious crime and only the one shooting. This was a tribute to the fast and very efficient way in which Waco administered the law, ably backed by Bix and Simon.

He was shaving when Bix opened his eyes and groaned, 'Can't you sleep none?'

'Not me,' replied Waco, eyeing the old deputy critically. 'I ain't old and with one foot in the grave.'

'Is that right,' growled Bix, fingering his whiskers tenderly. 'Waal, I never saw you do nothing to help me when I need it wust.'

'Not me. I've got more sense than tangle with two gals like that. I went for help, didn't I?'

Bix snorted. There'd been a fight between two drunken dance-hall girls outside the Guesthouse, and when Bix tried to separate them they had turned on him, both taking a healthy hold of his whiskers and yanking them hard. Waco took the easy way out; he went to the Twin Bridge and fetched along Molly, the tough lady bartender, who ended the fight by cracking the girls' heads together.

'Whyn't you go stop them, you was there first?'

'Me?' Waco replied, looking horrified. 'Why, it ain't fitting for the third deputy to take over from the first.' He paused, grinning broadly. 'It surely was a sight when they tailed down on your whiskers.'

Bix did not see the humour of the situation, nor did Simon, who scowled from under the blankets. He growled a plaintive desire to be let sleep until it was daylight and Bix snorted angrily.

'I surely hopes they feel as sore in the head as I feel in the whiskers.'

'There'll be some as'll say you should have brung Frank Derringer in, boy,' Simon remarked, sitting on the edge of the bed.

'Why? He was playing a fair game. The Judge told me to use my own judgement in cases like that, so I did. I've known ole Derry a long time and never once known him to cheat at cards.'

'How about that letter, boy?' Bix inquired. 'The stage'll be along there at about nine. Ole Axel, the driver, don't never run more than a couple of minutes late. It's one of the things he boasts about.'

'I'm going out there to take a look, be a fool not to.'

'Want one of us along?' asked Simon.

'Nope. It'll take both of you to tend to things here in town. There's only five in the gang and they'll likely not be hanging about and doing any fighting.'

With that, Waco slid his rifle from the saddleboot, cleaned it and slid a full twelve bullet load into the magazine. Next he cleaned and reloaded his matched Colts; if there was a fight he did not aim to be unprepared. After eating his breakfast he collected his big paint stallion and headed out of town. It was not much after seven o'clock and the town was silent, deserted, resting after the hectic previous night's celebrations.

Waco left town over the Colorado river bridge, behind Ella Baker's saloon. He saw a curtain at one of the upper windows draw aside but did not try and see who was watching him. He rode along the stage trail, keeping a careful watch around him. It could possibly be a trap, luring him away from town for an ambush, but he doubted it. Allowing the big paint to make a good pace Waco examined the land ahead of him. He'd ridden along the stage trail, exercising his horse, a couple of times since his arrival and knew the place well. It was the only one of its kind within three miles of the town and he'd looked it over once before as a possible place for a hold-up, discarding the idea as being too close to town.

The stage trail ran along the bottom of a valley, steep bush-and rock-covered sides rising up, offering good cover for a man or a gang of men. There was one place where the trail made a sharp blind turn which forced a coach to slow almost to a stop as it came around. That would be the place for the hold-up, Waco was sure of it. The coach would come around the corner slowly, the driver fully occupied with handling his team and the guard unable to see the trail ahead. He would be under the guns of the gang before he saw them. Then, if he was carrying passengers, he would be unable to fight without endangering them and no Wells Fargo guard would risk getting the passengers hurt. The young Texan was puzzled by the hold-up. There was something wrong with the whole set up. Ella Baker might have heard about it in her saloon, from a too-talkative member of the gang. Or there might be another reason behind the robbing of the stage. Suppose the hold-up was interrupted by Von Schnabel, broken up and the gang chased away. That would throw votes the German's way. In that case Von Schnabel would be on his way towards the place and Waco would not have a lot of time left to look the ground over and plan his moves.

Stopping his horse Waco looked around him. The men would halt the coach as it came around the corner. Von Schnabel's appearance would most probably be from the direction of the town, coming around the more gentle curve. His arrival would be the signal for the men to depart and that was the time of danger. The Wells Fargo guard was not going to miss a chance. Give him half a chance he would get either his shotgun or Colt into action. Which all pointed to one thing; the men were going to need to get away—fast. They would not go back towards town, riding by Von Schnabel, that would look suspicious. They might head around the blind corner the coach turned, but beyond it was a long, straight piece of trail which would throw them under fire of the guard if he went after them.

Then Waco saw it; a small path led up the slope away from the trail. It was only a narrow opening and a man entering it

51

would immediately be out of sight of the trail, hidden by the thick bush which grew on the slope. That was the escape route used by the men. It let them get out of sight quickly and wound up on to the open range. The guard would not be able to get a clear shot at the men as they rode along the narrow, winding path. Waco turned his horse, headed it for the path and started to ride up, eyes on the ground. Several horses had been ridden up the path on the previous day. There was a curve as soon as a man entered the narrow opening, and a bit further along, the trail widened out and Waco stopped the paint, and swung down to look around him with interest. He unstrapped his rope, tying one end to a tree, and making sure it was just the right height to catch a rider but miss the horse's head as it passed underneath. Carefully Waco led the rope to the ground, across the trail and out of sight into bushes at the other side. He went back and carefully hid the rope with leaves and dirt, then returned to take his horse off and leave it standing well hidden. He took the Winchester Centennial rifle from the boot and moved through the bushes until he found a place where he could look down on the trail, to where the hold-up would take place.

Getting down, Waco lined his rifle, caressed the trigger as if firing, then came to his feet and sprinted back to where he'd left the free end of his rope. He was sure that when the time came he would be able to make it. So he returned and settled down in the shelter of the bushes and waited with all the patience of a scalp-hunting Indian.

The sound of horses approaching brought him to the ready position, tense and watchful. There were five men riding around the gentle curve on the town side of the place. They wore cowhand rig and might have been anybody, cowhands on their way back to their spread; drifters looking for work. There was nothing about them to show what they were. The very ordinariness of the men was a pointer; there was nothing to show them out from any of the many cowhands who rode the cattle ranges from Texas to California, or from the Rio Grande to the Canadian border. Waco got the feeling they were his men. It grew even more so when he saw them halt their horses, dismount and one of their number go to the sharp corner to peer around it.

Still Waco made no move. There was no hurry, the coach was not here and so far there was nothing for him to move over. If he started shooting now the men would scatter. If he caught them he could not prove they were doing anything against the law.

One of the men glanced at a watch he took from his vest pocket, then nodded to the others. They pulled their bandanas up, masking the lower half of their faces, while their hat brims shielded their eyes. The look-out came back, nodded and mounted his horse. The rest all mounted, drawing their revolvers. Waco could hear the coach approaching. He lined the rifle, sliding the sight picture down to the body of one of the men, and focusing it on the ground beneath his horse's belly.

It was as neat a stage-coach hold-up as Waco could imagine. The coach came slowly around the corner and the guard found himself under the guns of the five men before he could hardly do more than draw breath. He tensed, hands gripping the wicked-looking ten-gauge shotgun, but there were passengers in the coach and he could not chance making a fight of it.

'Toss the scatter down!' shouted one of the masked men.

The shotgun clattered to the ground and the five men still sat their horses, not making any attempt to carry on with the robbery. The driver snorted angrily, not raising his hands, controlling his team.

'Git to it, damn ye!' he roared. 'I ain't never run late and I ain't wanting to start today.'

'Tough gent, huh?' scoffed the masked man. 'All right——'

Waco knew now that this was a grandstand play arranged for Von Schnabel. He could read that in the way the outlaws were acting. It was time he cut in, before Von Schnabel made his appearance. Somehow the German must be late.

Waco's rifle cracked, the bullet kicking dirt up under the feet of one of the horses. He sent another shot slamming behind a second man, saw the riders start to turn and the guard diving from the coach after his shotgun. Then Waco was up and running, throwing a shell into the breech of his rifle to replace the exploded case while he ran.

It was going to be close. Waco knew that as he raced to where he left his rope. There was barely time to rest his rifle against a bush, catch up the rope, jerk it tight and loop it around the trunk of a scrub oak. He didn't even have time to dally it, but braced his high heels and hung on.

The five men were coming fast. Too fast for them to be able to avoid the rope. The first man was swept from his saddle, rolling wildly to avoid being trampled on by the next horse. The second rider came down, the third saw the rope and tried to stop his horse but it was too late. The horse passed under the tight-stretched rope and the man gripped it, swinging from the saddle. His effort did him no good at all, for Waco released the end and the man fell on to his two friends. The other two managed to stop their horses but could neither get by their friends nor turn into the bush.

The language which came floating up was terrible to hear. Waco decided it was time to take control of the situation and restore peace and quiet. He picked up the rifle and left cover in a bound.

'Joke over!' he barked. 'Throw them high! Rangers here!'

It was a slip and he knew it as soon as he gave out the familiar challenge he'd so often used when riding for Captain Bertram C. Mosehan. The five men did not appear to notice how he worded his order. They saw the tall, fast-moving young Texan with the rifle and the deputy sheriff's badge, knowing they were caught. One of the five still needed convincing and learned, via a piece of lead weighing 405 grains and a bullet-busted shoulder, that a lined, cocked and ready Winchester ·45·75 rifle beat a holstered Colt revolver. More so when the Colt's user was lying on the ground and winded by his fall.

The rifle's lever was a blur of motion as Waco threw out the empty case and replaced it with a full load. He repeated his order and the men obeyed this time for they could see that they were matched with a master-hand. Waco stood ready, he heard excited shouts and running steps on the narrow path. The guard, driver and a couple of passengers came into sight, skidding to a halt as they saw the five men and the young Texan who'd captured them.

'Yowee!' whooped the driver. 'You ketched 'em, Drifter. Serves 'em right too. I ain't been late since me pet mule died in '73.'

'Pull their teeth for 'em,' Waco ordered, ignoring the praise.

54

'Swing down you pair and do it careful.'

The two men dismounted and the guard disarmed them, working in a way which showed he knew full well what he was doing. One of the passengers returned to the coach and brought a length of rope which was cut and used to secure the wrists of four of the outlaws. The fifth's wound was treated and rendered him incapable of causing any trouble at all. The masks were removed but none of the five men were known to Waco, yet the way they'd handled the hold-up showed they were not beginners at the work. One thing Waco noticed was that they were all light-haired men who appeared to be northerners, Norwegians, Danes, Germans or British. It did not strike him as being unusual at the moment. There was too much work to do for him to stand thinking about the gang. He whistled and his big paint came through the bush towards him; mounting, he rode after and brought back the three horses of the gang.

'May as well escort you to town, Drifter,' remarked the driver as they returned to the trail. 'They sp'iled me record, so there ain't no need for me to hurry any more.'

Von Schnabel rode slowly along the trail from Two Forks headed for the dry-wash. He consulted his watch and tried to time his arrival so that he would come on the scene at the right moment.

He sat his big roan stallion with stiff-backed grace, riding like a cavalry man and not with the relaxed, slouching ease of a cowhand. He'd left off his cutaway coat and wore a white shirt, European-style riding breeches, tucked into riding boots, which shone so as to reflect the surrounding scene. Across his saddle rested a magnificently checked and engraved Winchester rifle; but there was no sign of a hand-gun, either at his side or under his armpit.

According to his watch he'd plenty of time in hand. He held his horse to an even pace and thought of his plans. They were great plans and until the arrival of that damned Drifter Smith, were going along well. This business today was his last chance of pulling off the chore of County Sheriff. The young Texan's skilled handling of the law had lifted him well into public esteem, but there was just the slender chance that this hold-up would sway the vote back in Von Schnabel's favour.

Drifter Smith, if that was his name, would have made an ideal second-in-command, far better than Kyte, who was only in it for money. A man like Drifter Smith would serve loyally and with intelligence. There was no chance of getting the Texan to join, Von Schnabel knew that; a man like Drifter Smith did not change sides.

Von Schnabel snorted, he heard shots ahead and wondered if something had gone wrong, but did not urge his horse on at any better pace. The shots were distant and appeared to be from a rifle. His men were armed with revolvers and the Wells Fargo guard always used shotguns. It would probably be somebody hunting, or shooting with a new rifle. To make sure, the German glanced at his watch, it still wanted fifteen minutes for nine o'clock and the driver was known to hold his schedule.

So Von Schnabel rode on. His plans were big, too big for lesser men, but not for Count Ludwig Von Schnabel, late of His Prussian Majesty's Hussars. Those stupid fools who drove him from his fatherland, all over a duel where a Prince of the Blood died before Von Schnabel's sabre, would welcome him back with open arms when his great plan was brought to a successful conclusion. Kyte did not know what his plans were, nor did any other of his men; not even the five who were robbing, or pretending to rob, the coach, and they were the most loyal and trusted.

Von Schnabel brought his horse to a halt and stared ahead, blinking as if he could hardly believe his eyes. He stared at the stagecoach, harder at the five men who rode as prisoners before it, but hardest of all at the tall, handsome young Texan who rode by the side of the trail, his rifle resting on his hip as he watched the prisoners.

For all the rage which seethed inside him, Von Schnabel rode forward. To do otherwise would have been more than suspicious, for any man would show interest in such a sight. His eyes were on the five men as he approached, trying to give them a warning and an assurance that he would do what he could for them. The party came to a halt and he looked at Waco, asking:

'What's all this?'

'These five jaspers tried to relieve us of our wealth,' cackled the driver, before Waco could speak. 'But ole Drifter, he done stopped 'em.'

'Ketched 'em all. Wounded one,' the guard went on excitedly. 'I tell you, young Drifter here'll make the best damned sheriff this county——'

The words tailed off as the guard realised that he was talking to the other candidate for the post of county sheriff.

Von Schnabel ignored the words, turning his eyes to Waco. 'It would appear that you are always on hand at the right moment. How did you come to be riding out this way?'

'Just fortunate, I reckon,' drawled Waco, watching the prisoners. There was a slight change about them. They seemed to be sitting straighter in their saddles as Von Schnabel looked at them. Waco couldn't think where he'd seen men take such an attitude before. He knew he had, but could not just tie down where or when. 'This ole Dusty hoss of mine takes on airs something cruel if he don't get the bedsprings rid out of him regular.'

'And you just happened to be around here?'

'Why sure. Was cutting across country and saw this bunch looking all suspicious,' replied Waco, watching Von Schnabel's face now. 'So I just stuck in and took a hand. Got lucky and caught them all.'

Von Schnabel's face showed nothing of his thoughts. He did not believe the young Texan's presence was so easily explained away. Of late there had been too many things going wrong. Ella Baker knew too much of what was being planned in the Guesthouse Saloon, and Von Schnabel wondered who might be passing word to her. It might be nothing more than co-incidence, but he meant to be on his guard in future.

'We'd best get this lot to town, Drifter,' the guard remarked. 'I reckon you've got things to do when you get there.'

'Why sure,' agreed Waco. 'You coming in with us, Mr. Von Schnabel?'

'I may as well,' snapped the German, wanting to keep his eye on his men and let them know he would try to get them out of this trouble. He took out his watch and glanced at it. 'I thought you never ran either early or late, Axel.'

'Don't. 'Cepting that these ornery polecats delayed me.'

'But I make the time barely five minutes to nine,' objected

57

Von Schnabel.

The driver hauled out a battered old watch and studied it, then gave a delighted chuckle. 'Something must be wrong with that fancy watch of your'n. I makes it a quarter after.'

Von Schnabel frowned. He'd checked his watch with the big clock on the saloon before he left. They'd both showed the same time and he'd never thought to check on any other. He rode along behind the coach, scowling and almost black with rage. The rage did not decrease when he arrived in town and saw Drifter Smith getting acclaim for bringing in the men who'd tried to rob the stage. He could see now his plan was badly spoiled; he would have come in to be acclaimed merely for scaring the gang away. Drifter Smith stopped the hold-up and brought the gang in.

Silently he rode on to the Guesthouse and left his horse at the rail. Kyte was waiting for him, looking worried and with news which confirmed Von Schnabel's suspicions that there was a spy in his place.

'Boss, I found out after you'd left that somebody'd put back all the clocks down here twenty minutes.'

'I guessed that,' Von Schnabel replied. 'Send a man with my horse to the stable.'

He went to the bar-room beyond the batwing doors. Several of his workers lived above the saloon, as he did when not at his ranch. There were the four bartenders, three of the bouncers, a few of the gamblers and all the girls. It must be one of them, but which one? He remembered his coat had been hanging over the back of a chair, the watch in the fob pocket, while he took a bath after the saloon closed for the night.

'What're we going to do, boss?' Kyte asked.

'There is only one thing to do with a spy. Find out who is spying, who he, or she, spies for—and kill both.'

Down at the jail, Bix Smith and Simon could not have been more proud of Waco had he been their own flesh and blood. They put the prisoners into the cells, then Bix gave Waco some news which startled and worried him.

'Miz Ella wants you to come along to the Twin Bridge and make a speech to the folks who're there,' the old deputy drawled, grinning at Waco. 'I told her you'd be real pleased to.'

Waco growled a blanket curse which took in Bix, the entire Smith family and some left over for the wide-grinning Simon. There was no getting out of making the speech, unless a miracle happened and Waco felt that he was long out of miracles. He told the other two to let Ella know he'd be along after he'd washed and changed into a clean shirt. They left and Waco took his time, dragging out the washing as long as he could. Then he changed into a new shirt, but before he pinned the deputy's badge on he heard someone in the outer office and opened the door to see who it was.

'Howdy, ma'am,' he said, to the worried-looking towns-woman who stood in the office. 'Can I help you?'

'It's my little boy, Mr. Smith,' she replied. 'He went fishing on the other side of the Colorado River this morning and he isn't back yet.'

'I'll go and look for him right now, ma'am,' replied Waco eagerly, seeing a chance to avoid making the speech. 'Would you see that Bix gets to know about it. He's down to the Twin Bridge Saloon. Tell him I'll get back as soon as I can and make the speech.'

'Of course,' she replied. 'I'm meeting my husband there, we were going to hear what you had to say. Timmy went over the Colorado Bridge behind the saloon, he always goes that way, but I don't know if he went up or downstream.'

'Was he afoot, ma'am?'

'No, on his pony.'

'Then don't you worry none, ma'am,' replied Waco confidently. 'I'll find him for you.'

The woman watched Waco leave with some pride in her eyes. There was a good man; he was willing to go looking for her son when he should be making a vote-gathering speech. She aimed to see that everyone heard about it.

Waco was only too pleased to get out of making the speech and his departure from the town took on the aspect of a criminal sneaking away from his crime. He kept a wary eye on the Twin Bridge Saloon as he rode behind it, heading across the Colorado River bridge and looking for some sign of the youngster's passing. He had no trouble in finding the tracks of the pony, they were the only set on the side of the river. He was even more sure when, after riding some way down stream, he found a fishing pole resting against the tree. The youngster did not appear to have been lucky in his fishing and must have taken a ride. Waco followed the tracks, finding where the youngster hid behind a bush.

The tracks started off across country, the youngster apparently playing at some game, for there was evidence that he kept to cover and frequently stayed hidden for some moments before moving on again.

A faint, distant chattering sound brought Waco to a halt. He sat his horse without moving for a time, trying to locate where the sound came from. He heard it again, right off in the distant hills. The sound was somehow strange, yet appeared to strike a chord in his memory. He rode forward slowly, still watching the tracks and listening. There was one more burst of that chattering noise and Waco frowned. Apart from the distance it was away the sound might have been the warning buzz of a rattlesnake. Waco was almost sure he'd heard the sound before, but his tenacious memory could not remember where or when.

The youngster seemed to be wandering on for miles. Waco was alert for he'd seen fairly recent grizzly bear signs and the big bear was not the sort of thing for a boy to run into. Trailing was slow work, the ground not helping Waco to make fast time. It was almost four o'clock in the afternoon when he brought his horse to a halt behind a bush and waited to see who, or what, was coming through the thick cover towards him. Gun in hand, Waco waited, then sent his horse jumping out to confront a youngster riding a tired-looking pony.

'Yipe!' yelled the youngster, reining in and looking more than a little scared by the sudden appearance.

'Hold hard, boy,' said Waco soothingly. 'I'm sorry if I scared you, but I reckon you're a lil mite offen your range.'

'Gosh-a-mighty, Drifter,' replied the youngster. 'I thought you was one of them Injuns I saw.'

'Injuns, huh?' Waco replied, grinning now. The youngster must have been playing a game, pretending he was an Army scout and trailing hostile Indians. It was a game Waco remembered playing when he was a boy about this age, in the Ranse River country of Texas. The boy here must have become so absorbed in his game that he just kept moving on, then finally, turned to head for home. He could be looking scared because he thought he'd gotten himself lost, for there was a real fear about him which showed plain enough to the young Texan: 'Which tribe was they, *amigo*? Sioux, Cheyenne, Ute, Apache?'

The boy looked back nervously over his shoulder and licked his lips. Waco was more puzzled than ever. The youngster was plainly scared but his imagination, due to being lost, might be playing tricks on him. His pony must have been headed for home, using the inborn instinct of a range horse to head back for its stable.

'I surely don't know what tribe they was, Drifter,' he finally replied. 'But there was eight or more of them with that mean ole buffalo-hunter who sometimes hangs about with Matt Kyte.'

CHAPTER SEVEN

BETH MORROW COMES TO TOWN

It was shortly after noon that Beth Morrow came in sight of the town of Two Forks. She rode the dainty dun gelding with the easy grace of a cowhand, matched the skill of the half-dozen hard-riding men who surrounded her. She was on her way to town for the election. Her BM crew were the last to be heading for town. Having only just ended their round-up and being one of the further ranches of the county, they'd not been able to make it before.

The men who rode around her were a typical batch of cowhands; hard-riding, hard-working and hard-playing men, loyal to the brand they rode for and more than loyal to their beloved boss lady. They rode with her, argued with her, laughed at her jokes and would have laid down their lives for her any time it was needed.

There might have been prettier girls, more intelligent girls, girls with more talent than Beth Morrow, but to even hint so in front of the ranch crew meant fighting the bunch of them.

She made a good picture, sitting astride on the back of the dun gelding, her long black hair held back with a red band, the Stetson hat hanging by its storm strap. She wore a tartan shirtwaist, blue jeans and dainty, high-heeled cowhand boots with spurs on the heels. It was a style of dress which set off her full and willowy figure.

Beth was worth a second look in any company. Her face was gentle and very beautiful. The eyes were dark and seemed to glow with a rich joy of life. The nose was small, well shaped and the mouth red-lipped, full, yet never feeling any kind of cosmetic, or needing it. It was a face of unspoiled beauty, unaided charm, a sweet, kind and gentle face.

Beth's foreman, tough, middle-aged, craggy Seth Braden,

was proud of her as he watched her from the corner of his eye, listening to her arguing with the hands. The girl could manage to be friend, sister and confidante to the hands and still be their boss, handling them with easy assurance.

'What you aiming to do when we hit town?' Braden asked, cutting across a long argument as to who ate the most pie in some contest they held.

'See Bix and Simon first off,' she replied. 'It's about time those two old villains earned their pay and stopped us losing cattle.'

'We don't need no lawman to do that,' whooped a dark-looking young man by the name of Nakton White. 'Just you say the word and we'll head over there and take them Mormons to pieces and get back all our stock.'

Beth surveyed the cowhand with disgust, then turned to the others. 'Hasn't Darkie got a brain? He's a regular Pinkerton sneak. He knows it's the Mormons taking off with our stock.'

'Waal, I got it on real good authority. Right smart from that tough Mr. Jack Hatch, hisself,' replied Darkie, when the jeers of the others died down. 'He allows it's them, so it must be.'

'Hatch talks too much,' Beth said quietly.

Braden nodded his agreement. He thought of the tall, handsome, dandified cowhand he took on to help with the round-up. The man was a real good worker, but a loud-mouthed trouble-causer and not the sort Braden cared for. That was the reason Braden left the man back at the BM house, with two of the old BM hands he could trust. When the trip was over, Braden aimed to change a horse in Hatch's saddle string, giving the man notice that he was no longer welcome on the ranch.

'You want for me to fire him?' he asked the girl.

'Was we to fire every hand who talks too much we wouldn't have any of this worthless crew left,' replied Beth.

The jeers and some of the comments thrown back at Beth would have given any stranger who did not know cowhands the idea that they were a poor mannered bunch. If the same stranger had dared to say half of the things to the girl he would have rapidly learned that the cowhands were exercising their rights as old friends.

Darkie White came alongside the girl and started to give out with large chunks of his wisdom, so she kicked his mean-look-ing horse in the ribs. The horse left the ground with a wild busking bound which almost landed Darkie on the ground and took some handling to get it back under control.

With a laugh Beth looked back to where, in the distance, the BM chuckwagon was following them, driven by the cook and coming to town for supplies. She put the petmakers to her dun's sides, sending the little horse racing towards the cattle bridge over the Colorado River. The rest of the crew, not to be outdone, sent their cowhorses hurling after the girl, riding with the centaur-like skill of the cowhand. They thundered over the bridge, on to Colorado Street, whooping, yelling and firing their revolvers into the air. It was nothing more than the usual way a ranch crew came to town, letting everyone know they'd arrived.

Beth brought her horse to a halt and the rest of the crew, red-faced and laughing, brought their horses sliding to a stop around her.

'I'll be headed back for home soon after dark,' she told the grinning cowhands. 'I don't want to be gone too long, what with the cattle we've been losing. I don't reckon any of you'll be ready to come, though.'

'Not us,' Angus McKie, the ranch's poker champion replied. 'We don't aim to head back until we're busted clear through the blanket.'

'Which same won't be long if there's a halfway good poker player in town,' scoffed Beth. 'Don't you bunch go drinking the Twin Bridge Saloon dry.'

For all the banter, the cowhands and Beth knew they would go back to the ranch as a bunch, the same way they came to town. They would have taken their fill of city life by the time Beth was ready to go back home.

Beth watched the cowhands heading away, a tolerant smile on her face. None of her crew were heavy drinkers and would be capable of riding back to the BM under their own power. She was a true western girl, despite the fact that she'd been well educated in the east. She never forgot what the Morrows (she'd never known her parents, having been brought up on the BM by an aunt and uncle) had taught her; a saloon was not a place of evil, it was necessary. She knew there were bad saloons, she also knew that the Twin Bridge Saloon was not one of these and it was the favourite place for her crew. She knew the saloon women supplied a need in the west, as did the other women, not necessarily the same as the saloon girls, who worked the houses of the red lamp.

Beth swung from her saddle and looked at the two big posters outside the jail. She had not known that any other candidate than Von Schnabel was on hand for the election but could see there was now. Von Schnabel's poster was big and blared out the message of his intention to clean out Two Forks. The other poster was just as large and glaring, but she'd never heard the name before.

'DRIFTER SMITH FOR SHERIFF,' she read, then mused aloud, 'Now who is Drifter Smith? I've never heard of him before.'

She opened the jail office door and heard Bix Smith airing his views about the candidate for sheriff.

'Dagnab that damned, no-good yahoo,' he growled. 'Done snuck off after that kid rather than come in and make a speech.'

'Thought you done well at it, though,' Simon replied, then he looked at the door. A beam of delight came to his face as he swung his feet from the desk top and stood up. 'Howdy Miss Beth, howdy. You brought your boys in to vote for Wa— Drifter Smith?'

'I don't know?' she replied, smiling back. 'Who is he?'

Bix Smith looked straight at the girl. 'As square, fair and good a man as ever drawed breath, Miss Beth.'

Beth looked hard at the old-timer. She'd never heard him sound so eager about any man he ever worked under, even the legendary Dragoon Dune, of whom Bix would never hear of a better. Now it seemed that Dragoon Dune had a man who was at least his equal in Bix Smith's book.

'Better than old Dragoon Dune?' she asked mischievously.

Bix coughed, not wishing to be trapped in such a manner. 'He ain't all that old, but he packs a world of savvy. I've never seen a better man with a gun. Not real recent anyways.'

'He chased Matt Kyte and four more gunhands out of the Twin Bridge,' Simon went on. 'Then backed down a tough drunk who was shooting Colorado Street up, took his guns and knives offen him without even drawing on him. Then he stopped a big bunch of Mormons from raising hell in town and made their Bishop sing low. There was a young gunhand got drunk and had a gun on Drifter, and ole Drifter took him. Then put that killer Keg Bullock under, and run Dillis out of town. He's done plenty to tame this town down now. The cowhands like him, he gets on with them.'

'Shucks, Simon. You all forgetting about this morning,' interrupted Bix.

'This morning?' Beth smilingly asked. 'What did this wonder man do this morning, after all that?'

'Why, he heads out along the stage trail and stops a hold-up, brings in the five owlhoots. Then he's supposed to come along to the Twin Bridge Saloon and make him a fancy speech to the folks, but Mrs. Schulze comes in and says her lil boy's lost. So ole Drifter just says "to hell with speechifying, even if I lose votes". And he heads out to find the button.'

The girl laughed. Any man who could bring out such admiration from this pair of hardened old-timers was a man to be reckoned with. She formed an idea that Drifter Smith was a hard, tough lawman in his early thirties, the sort who made a living running the tough towns.

'He sounds quite a man. Do you think he can get who ever it is who's stealing my stock?'

'Why surely so,' agreed Bix with complete confidence. 'He'll make a start on it as soon as he can. You should come in later on and see him.'

'I'll do just that,' she promised. 'Don't worry. The BM vote's going to your friend, Drifter Smith.'

The girl left the jail, making her way through the streets and meeting several people she knew. She was stopped and heard plenty about Drifter Smith. Her idea of what he must look like did not change, even though several of her girl friends were all talking about how handsome Drifter Smith was. Strangely, not one person mentioned that he was a Texan. For all that, the people in town, the ones she talked with, appeared to be sure that Drifter Smith would make them a real good county sheriff. By the time Beth visited the Trenard store and ordered her supplies she was sure that he was the man for her.

Nightfall found Beth standing by the wagon looking around

for the members of her ranch crew. She'd been along to the jail and recorded her vote earlier in the day, but the famous Drifter Smith was not back from looking for the little boy and she had not yet seen him.

Beth stood by the wagon for fifteen minutes or so, then decided it was time she went to find her missing crew. She walked along the street and came to a halt at the corner of the Guesthouse. For a time she stood looking across at the Twin Bridge Saloon, then crossed over. She stopped by the window and looked in. She'd never been so close to the Twin Bridge Saloon before and was suddenly filled with desire to see what was on the other side of the swinging doors. Her every instinct warned her not to be silly; the good women of the town did not enter a saloon when it was open for business. The women inside would resent her presence, for inside the saloon was their province, they stayed off the street and expected the same courtesy to be extended by the townswomen.

For a moment she stood looking at the batwing doors, then drew in a deep breath and stepped forward. She pushed open the doors and moved into the bar-room of the saloon, looking around with considerable interest. The crowd appeared to be enjoying themselves but she could see nothing to offend her, things appeared to be as quiet and well-behaved as a church social. Her eyes went to a table in the centre of the room, her foreman, the foremen of three of the local spreads and a good-looking woman were playing poker. Beth started towards the table; she knew the woman was the owner, Ella Baker, for she'd seen her around town.

'Seth. Let's go after this hand.'

The words brought every eye from the table to the girl. Ella gasped, her face lost colour and her hands crumpled the cards she held. Seth Braden and the other three men stared at the girl and the BM hands at the nearby tables gave startled exclamations as they saw their boss-lady in the saloon.

Before any of the card players could say anything, Beth felt a hand on her sleeve and a voice said, 'All right, girlie, out!'

Turning, Beth found herself facing a girl her own size, a tanned girl with short, boyishly cut hair. The girl's face looked vaguely familiar and Beth frowned, seeing the man's clothes and the gun. She turned back and spoke to Braden.

'Are you ready, Seth?'

Lynn Baker frowned, catching Beth's arm and turning her. 'I said out, girlie!' she snapped.

'Make me!' hissed Beth, suddenly angry that this girl should try and push her around.

Ella came to her feet, trying to prevent trouble, but she was too late. Lynn dropped her hand, the gun lifting clear of the holster but she did not bring the Colt to line. Even before her mother let out a scream of: 'Drop it', Lynn was already releasing her grip of the butt.

Beth grabbed the other girl's wrist, lifting it and banging it down on her knee as she'd seen the hands do in play at the spread. She felt the gun fall free and pushed the other girl backwards. Lynn staggered slightly and with a wild yell hurled herself forward, hands digging into Beth's long hair and tearing at it. Beth let out a yell of anger mingled with pain, her own hands tangled with the short cropped black hair on Lynn's head and they reeled backwards.

Leaping up, Ella came around the table fast, knocking aside one of her girls who came running to help Lynn. Then she made towards the wild tangle of arms, legs and thrashing, writhing bodies of the fighting girls. Braden caught her arm, holding her back.

'Easy, Ella,' he growled. 'You'll have a riot on your hands if you try and stop them. It's Beth's fault, she shouldn't have come here.'

'Yahoo!' howled Darkie White as Beth swung a wild slap which staggered Lynn across the room. 'Up the BM.'

The girls met again, tangling like two enraged wildcats. They tripped and crashed to the floor, rolling over and over, swinging wild slaps and waving their legs as they fought. They screamed in anger, squealed as a fist landed, each struggling to try and pin the other girl down. Lynn was used to tangling with tough saloon girls, she expected no trouble in dealing with this girl from outside. She found her mistake fast enough for Beth, despite her upbringing and eastern schooling, was just as strong and fit as Lynn herself. She'd learned how to take care of herself in her tomboy childhood and in the wild tangle gave as good as she got.

The entire crowd in the saloon, even the hardened drinkers,

formed a large circle around the fighting girls, yelling their approval and encouragement. The cowhands were almost all rooting for Beth. She was one of them and they wanted to see her hand the other girl her needings. The saloon girls were just as wildly cheering Lynn, hoping to see the townswoman who'd trespassed on their domain beaten.

The two girls rolled apart and forced themselves to their feet, standing with legs braced apart, hair dishevelled and gasping for breath.

'Had enough?' gasped Lynn, hitching up her pants.

Beth licked the blood which trickled from the side of her mouth. Then she swung a wild punch which staggered Lynn backwards into the bar. Lynn hung there for a moment and as Beth came to her, lowered her head to butt into her and resume the wild fight. They reeled backwards, fighting just as wildly as before and went down again, neither able to gain any advantage over the other.

Big Molly, one of the bartenders, forced her way to Ella's side, watching the exhausted girls for a moment, then asked : 'Want me to stop them?'

'You try and you'd have all the cowhands to deal with,' replied Ella. She saw Bix Smith and Simon Girty in the crowd and shook her head in answer to the unspoken word of the old first deputy.

Lynn and Beth were on their feet now, struggling weakly as they staggered backwards. Lynn felt herself hit the edge of a table; Beth was pushing swinging slaps at her face and, trying to avoid punishment, Lynn went backwards on to the table top. Beth's reaction was automatic and instinctive. She lunged on to the table, on top of Lynn, trying to bang the other girl's head against the hard wood. Beth was exhausted, she could hardly breathe and the other girl's face appeared to be whirling before her eyes. She felt Lynn struggle weakly beneath her, then she rolled off and Lynn was throwing a leg astride her. With the last of her strength Beth twisted Lynn from her. Locked in each other's arms they rolled across the top of the table.

Seeing what was going to happen, Ella started forward. She was too late, for the girls rolled off the table and crashed to the floor. They lit down side by side and came apart, flopping on to their backs, then laying still. Apart from the heaving of their breasts, neither girl made a move; they'd been all but exhausted on the table and the fall finished the fight.

Ella was the first to get to the girls. She dropped on to her knees and looked down nervously at each of them in turn, showing as much concern over Beth as she did over Lynn. She looked up at Braden, who was by her side, and there was something like relief on her face. She'd seen cat-fights in plenty while running a saloon and knew that neither girl was seriously hurt. They'd both got the makings of a black eye, a bloody nose and a swollen lip, but there was no serious injury. Tenderly she pulled Beth's torn-open shirt together and then looked at the cheering, wildly excited crowd. There was one way of getting rid of them and she took it.

'Drinks on the house, Madge. Belly up to the bar and drink to a pair of real game gals, boys!'

The words brought the desired result, there was a rush for the bar. A few of the saloon girls gathered around and one looked at the dirty, sweat-streaked and buised faces.

'They look a helluva lot alike,' she said.

Ella stared at the girl and there was real fear in her eyes. 'Get among the crowd, you bunch!' she ordered. 'Keep them talking.'

The girls went, not knowing what brought on a sudden hard note in their boss's voice and put it to her worry about the fight. Ella let out a long sigh, then looked at Seth Braden as he bent over Beth.

'Poor lil Beth,' he said gently. 'She'll be stiff'n a dead polecat tomorrow morning. I'll put her in the back of the wagon and get her home.'

'Keep her in town,' Ella suggested.

'Nope,' replied Braden, picking the girl up, then calling for the rest of the BM hands. 'See you next time I come in, Ella.'

Ella nodded in reply, then told Big Madge to help Lynn to her room. The big blonde woman lifted Lynn up and made her way across the room to the stairs which led to the upper part of the building.

'That gal of your'n sure can fight, Ella,' whooped one of the men who'd been in the card game with her.

'Yes, they can,' replied Ella, then stopped, her face even

more pale.

However, the man did not appear to have noticed the way she put the words and turned to the card table once more. Her attention was no longer on the game, for she was worried. The girl's remark, or her own slip of the tongue, almost brought out Ella's secret, the secret that not even Lynn shared with her.

Before the fight could be discussed too much there was a more than welcome interruption. The local Judge came in with the news that Drifter Smith was elected sheriff with a large majority. There was only one snag now, the young Texan was not back from searching for the boy. If he was, he had not made his appearance at the saloon. Bix slipped out, at Ella's suggestion, to head for the jail and see if he could find the youngster.

The jail office was empty, but when Bix opened the door of the living quarters, he saw something which worried him, Waco's gunbelt, with the matched, staghorn-butted Colts, lay on the bed with his star. There was no sign of him, nor had there been his big paint outside. Thinking the young Texan might be tending to his horse, Bix looked out back, his eyes going to the horses belonging to the five hold-up men, in the civic pound. Waco's big paint stallion did not take kindly to strange horses, so the young Texan might have taken the horse to the livery barn for the night. It was unusual for him to walk the streets without his gunbelt, but he did have his rifle and the barn was not far enough away.

Bix checked on his prisoners, then headed back to the Twin Bridge Saloon. He walked in and immediately Molly, one of the bartenders, came forward. 'Ella'd like to see you in the office, Bix,' she said.

Bix went to the small side room Ella used as an office. He knocked and opened the door. The moment he stepped inside he knew there was something badly wrong. It showed on Simon's face and on Ella's. Bix could never remember when he had seen her so worried.

'Is he there?' Ella asked.

'Nope, his gunbelt's on the bed. I figger he's gone to the livery barn with his hoss——'

'He's in trouble!' Ella interrupted. 'Wharton shot him, his

horse carried him out of town.'

'*What!*' bellowed Bix. 'I'll go out there'n' I'll tear Wharton's heart out with my bare hands.'

'Sit down and keep quiet!' Ella ordered, knowing the old deputy was real likely to do just what he said. 'You can't do Waco any good tonight. I don't know for certain what's happened. Listen, at dawn tomorrow I want you to take out and try to trail Waco. I'll fix it that if he's hurt, or you can't find him, there will be a letter from him, explaining why he's not here. I'll want the jail log again to do it.'

'Go git it,' Bix ordered and Simon left the room, headed for the jail. Bix went on: 'How'd you get to know, Ella?'

'A friend told me Wharton came to the Guesthouse in a hurry and told Kyte, who called Von Schnabel over and told him.'

Bix asked no more questions. He knew Ella would never tell him who the friend was and did not blame her. Whoever it was who worked for Ella at the Guesthouse Saloon was taking a big chance. One slip would mean almost certain death.

The old deputy was worried. The previous sheriff was murdered and they'd never been able to find the man who did the killing. Now Waco might also be dead.

Ella was a worried woman as she made the arrangements for the forged letter to be written. Waco might be dead, it was likely he was. If so she would have to try and stall Von Schnabel as long as she could. It might be that she would have to do as her daughter wished, call on Butch Cassidy to help her out.

The office door opened and Lynn limped in. The girl's face was washed and no longer bleeding but her right eye was a beautiful shiner. She'd tucked her shirt into her trousers again but had not changed.

Lynn looked distinctly uneasy, she knew her mother did not like cat-fights or trouble in the saloon and expected a severe bawling out. 'I'm sorry, maw,' she said contritely. 'Who was she?'

'Your—a girl who owns a ranch in the back country,' Ella replied.

'I couldn't lift my gun against her, maw. I don't know why, but I couldn't do it.'

Ella slipped an arm around her daughter's shoulders, squeezing her gently. 'I'm pleased you didn't, dear. Now you get to your room, have a bath and go to bed.'

Lynn left the room and Bix Smith entered, followed by Frank Derringer, the gambler. He smiled a greeting, then the smile died as he saw that this was more than a social call. He knew Ella too well to think otherwise; the woman was clearly worried and he'd played poker with her enough to know how good a poker-face she possessed. He took the chair Ella indicated and sat back.

'How well do you know Drifter Smith, Frank?' asked Ella.

'You mean Waco, don't you?' he replied.

'We mean Waco,' agreed Ella, cutting through Bix's angry growl.

'I served as a special deputy with him under Dusty Fog in Mulrooney. Taught him some about cards. We're old friends. I didn't let on we knew each other. I'd heard about that trouble down in Arizona and didn't want to tip his hand. Couldn't say I knew him, not after he didn't take me in for killing that cardshark.'

'He's in trouble,' said Ella.

The relaxation left Derringer and he sat up straight, his face suddenly hard and cold. 'Tell it, ma'am,' he snapped.

Ella told all she knew, the gambler not speaking until she finished, then growling out a threat to kill Wharton on sight. Ella shook her head :

'That won't help, or I'd do it myself.'

'I heard shooting, was playing in a big stake game along at the Hotel,' Derringer remarked. 'I'll start playing at the Guesthouse from now on, see if I can get some certain proof. There'll be three men coming along. If anything happened to the boy, they'll just about tear this town apart, board by board.'

'Who do you mean?' asked Ella.

'Dusty Fog, Mark Counter and the Ysabel Kid. Waco's closer'n any brother to them three and they'll be here as soon as they get word. They'll just about tear Two Forks into lil pieces if they don't get the right answers.'

Bix left the office and headed for the jail. He found Simon with disturbing news. The five prisoners had obtained a key to the cell and were gone. The old deputy cursed savagely, but there was nothing much he could do.

The following morning, Von Schnabel and several cronies arrived breathing fire and smoke over the escape of the prisoners. The German's insistence on seeing the new sheriff was answered by Bix handing him a sheet of paper. The German began to read and his face showed a mixture of anger and disbelief.

'Bix,' he read. 'Heard I was elected sheriff. I'm headed out for the range, want to take a look around and see about this rustling that's going on. I'll see you in a week or so. Take care of the town and don't let any gals get hold of your whiskers while I'm gone.'

He compared the writing on the paper with the entry on the page of the jail log, recording Waco's finding of the boy and return to town, then departure to investigate the rustling. The writing was identical, that he was sure of.

So Von Schnabel was left with no option but to take the word of the letter. He could not announce that one of his men claimed to have bushwacked and run the new sheriff out of town. He tried to stir up public opinion over the escape of the five men, but most folks were inclined to scoff at it. The men had taken nothing in the hold-up, were not badly wanted elsewhere, so their escape saved the county the cost of a trial. Folks regarded Waco's disappearance as yet another proof of their new sheriff's willingness to get on with his work. They thought he was giving good value for his money.

A week passed slowly by, the town remained quiet, held down by a rejuvenated pair of tough deputies. Frank Derringer played in the games at the Guesthouse, his eyes often on Matt Kyte, who was by now almost always accompanied by Ben Wharton.

The town was quiet, to most people it was peaceful and calm. To Ella Baker, Frank Derringer and the two deputies it was merely the lull before the storm broke.

CHAPTER EIGHT

BETH MORROW HELPS A STRAY

It was dark when Waco and the boy rode over the bridge behind the Twin Bridge Saloon. The young Texan was deeply puzzled and worried. His mind was still busy trying to connect that strange, distant chattering sound with what he'd seen. The boy was very hungry, he'd also tired his horse and so Waco was forced to stay out on the range for a time. He'd shot and cooked a rabbit for them, then made a check on the story of the Indians. He found the new tracks of a bunch of horses, at least ten or so he made it. The thing which worried him was that only one of the horses was shod.

The office was deserted when Waco arrived. He'd hoped to find one of the deputies with whom he could discuss what he'd heard and found out. The street was quiet, a few people moving around but no one he could recognise and ask about Bix or Simon.

Stripping off his gunbelt, Waco went into the living quarters at the rear, hoping that one of the deputies would be there. He could see no sign of them and so left his gunbelt and the deputy's badge lying on his bed while he went to tend to his horse.

Waco rode his paint around the side of the jail and brought it to a halt by the civic pound. He swore under his breath as he saw the five horses, belonging to the men he'd arrested in the morning, standing in the corral. The big paint was not the kind of animal to take kindly to sharing a corral with strange horses and there would be trouble if Waco left it with the others. He sighed, it would be easy enough to take the horse to the livery barn and leave it for the night.

For a moment Waco thought of going inside and strapping on his guns, but decided against it. He'd got the rifle in the saddleboot and a box of ·45·75 shells in his pocket, that would be all the armament he needed. So he rode the horse along the back street, headed for the livery barn.

Some instinct made Waco turn in his saddle. He saw a dark shape coming from a side turning. The shape looked familiar, Waco's turn saved his life for the man held a gun. Flame lashed from the barrel towards Waco, even as he was bending for the rifle. He felt a searing pain across the side of his head and slid forward along the paint's neck. Another shot flamed out, the bullet hissing close over the young Texan's head. Instantly the big paint was running, carrying its master away from the dangerous area; luck, pure blind luck the only thing keeping Waco in the saddle. The man who'd done the shooting started to sprint after the horse, saw it thunder over the Colorado River and stood listening to the fast fading beat of the paint's hooves. Then he turned and slouched back towards the busy Colorado Street, coming into the light from a saloon window. Ben Wharton stood in the light for a moment, a grin on his face. He'd seen that damned Drifter Smith riding towards him and took a chance on getting him. The Texan must be either dead or badly injured, that was for sure. If he'd only been grazed, or the bullet had missed, he'd not have run but would have been throwing lead back with both hands.

Out on the range the big paint finally halted, standing snorting in the dark. Waco still lay across the horse's neck, then slowly he slid down and fell to the ground. The huge paint stood like a statue over its master for a long time. At last Waco started to drag himself to his feet. He groaned and put a hand to his head, feeling the rough dry blood which smeared his face. Weakly he dragged himself back on to the horse's saddle and sat for a moment looking around him in a dazed manner as if he did not know where he was. The world appeared to be roaring around him and he started the paint walking towards where, in the distance, he saw the flickering light of a camp fire. The paint walked on, moving carefully, as if it was trying to avoid jolting him. Waco clung on, the fire was getting closer. He'd a blurred impression of people around the fire, then everything went black again.

Beth Morrow groaned as she climbed from the back of the BM

wagon. She was stiff, sore, her hair felt as if the roots were on fire and every muscle ached. She limped towards the fire and the ranch crew watched her with some concern.

'How're you feeling, Beth gal?' Braden asked and nodded to the cook who brought a box for her to sit on.

'I thought it was a fair fight,' she replied, managing to smile. 'Then she hit me with something hard and that's all I can remember. What'd she hit me with, a chair?'

'The floor,' replied Darkie with a grin.

Beth sank on to the box, ruefully touched her swollen right eye and winced to the delight of the watching hands. She did not meet Braden's accusing eyes for Beth was feeling ashamed of herself. She was in the wrong in going into the Twin Bridge Saloon and honest enough to admit it. However, she'd been the spread's representative in the fight and did not like to think that she'd let the brand down by being beaten by the other girl.

'Sure was a fair whirl, Beth,' whooped another of the hands. 'Even if it did come out a stand-off.'

'A stand-off?' she asked, looking at the grinning faces around her. 'But I thought I lost.'

'Ran a draw,' Braden replied. 'You both fell off that table and were too tuckered out to go on.'

She watched her foreman's face, reading the worry on it and forming the wrong idea of why he was worried. The other hands started to prepare their bedrolls for spending the night on the range, as they'd left town far later than they aimed to do.

'Don't you worry, Seth,' she said warmly. 'Mrs. Baker won't hold it against you for what happened.'

'What do you mean, gal?' Braden growled.

'I've heard the boys joshing you about going to see her every time you go into town. You never use any other saloon.'

'I like the Twin Bridge,' said Braden, flushing slightly. 'It's as near a clean and honest place as you could find anywheres at all. Mrs. Baker's a real lady and there's plenty in town who owe her a lot.'

'Who was the girl I fought with?' asked Beth. 'I don't know, but I'm sure I've seen her before, that I should know her.'

'That was Lynn, Mrs. Baker's gal.'

'She shouldn't have tried to pull a gun on me. That was why I got riled. I caught her before she could lift it.'

Braden did not reply. He'd seen that Lynn was not even trying to lift the gun, that she'd been about to drop it, even before Beth attacked her. He was about to remark on the subject when he heard a distant sound. His hand dropped to his hip and loosened the low-hanging Colt gun as he heard the sound of a horse approaching.

The cowhands heard the sound at the same time, coming to their feet and all reaching for their guns. No man approached a fire without announcing his arrival with a call for permission to come in, not unless he was looking for trouble, or was badly hurt.

A big paint stallion walked into the light of the fire, its rider hanging forward, arms dangling on either side of the sleek neck. Beth started forward but Braden was in front of her, his gun out, ready for any trick. He lowered the rider to the ground and the others gathered around.

'What is it?' asked Beth.

'Looks like he's been shot,' replied Braden, then looked at the cook. 'What you reckon, Cookie?'

The cook, who also handled any rough doctoring on the spread, bent forward, looking down at the wound. He grunted; the man had been lucky, very lucky. The bullet grazed the side of his head, opening a furrow which was shallow, bloody, but not over dangerous.

'How is he, Cookie?' Beth asked worriedly. 'Take him by the fire. Darkie, make a bed up for him, will you?'

The man moved fast, obeying the girl's orders. Waco was carried to the side of the fire and laid on the blankets Darkie put down. Beth bent forward and took the Stetson off, it had been hanging back by the storm strap when Waco was shot and was still slung behind his back. She looked down at the face; it was so young, strong and handsome. There was something like a lump in the girl's throat as she looked at the wound. An inch the other way and this handsome young man would be dead.

'I wonder who he is,' she said, as the cook started to clean the wound.

Braden did not reply. He could never remember seeing her

78

look in such a way at any man. He looked down at the Texan's boots, then at the hat. Both were costly, the hat a genuine J.B. Stetson, not a cheap woolsey; the boots were costly, made-to-measure. His clothes were good quality and the shirt looked new. There was some of the signs of a top-hand about this young man. He was not wearing a gunbelt but the levis showed one was mostly strapped around the lean waist. Braden's keen eyes noticed something more sinister than just a gunbelt. There were signs of two holsters and the bottoms of the holsters were tied down when he wore them. It was an old range saying that a man who tied down his holster did not talk much with his mouth.

The angry snort of a horse brought Beth and Braden's eyes back to the big paint stallion. One of the hands was walking towards it, meaning to tend to it. The paint snorted and Beth called.

'Keep back from him, Johnny.'

The cowhand did not need that warning. He knew a bad horse when he saw one and here stood a real bad horse. Beth came to her feet and walked towards the big horse, speaking softly and soothingly to it.

'Watch him, Beth gal,' warned Braden, dropping his hand to his gun butt.

The girl did not stop, but walked straight up to the big paint, never showing any hesitation and talking all the time. The horse snorted again but slowly it relaxed and allowed the girl to reach out a hand and touch its neck. Its head dropped and snuffled at her shirt and she stroked its neck. Then she started to work the saddle loose. She could handle a saddle, even the unfamiliar double-girthed rig every Texas man used. When the horse was cooled she stripped the saddle and bridle off, allowing the paint to move away and graze.

Braden came to the girl's side, his eyes went to the saddle. 'No bedroll on it,' he remarked. 'You aiming to tote him out to the spread with us?'

'I am!' replied Beth defiantly.

'We don't know him, gal.'

'He's hurt. That's all that matters.'

Braden's hard face relaxed, he laid his horny hand on her head and gently ruffled her hair.

'You allus bringing some damned fool hurt thing back to home,' he said softly. 'Remember that time you found that wolf pup and toted it in. Fed it for a month and then it bit your hand.'

Beth looked from Braden to Waco's still form. She shook her head. 'Not this one, Seth. He's not wearing guns.'

'Has been, and regular. Look at his hands. They've got the marks of a gun-using man on them. Got the marks of a rope, too,' Braden replied, bending to pull the Winchester from the saddleboot. 'One of the new'ns. A forty-five-seventy-five.'

Beth nodded her agreement. It was the first time she'd seen one of the new Winchester Centennial rifles. They were little used by cowhands for they were expensive, more so than the lighter Model of '73 or '66 which the cowhands preferred. The Centennial's ammunition gave a greater range, but was more costly than the bullets for either the Centrefire '73, or the Rimfire '66. The Winchester found favour among the visiting hunters, but only two kinds of Western men carried it for the extra range, Lawmen—and outlaws.

'He could have bought it any place,' she snapped, eyeing her foreman truculently. 'It doesn't prove anything.'

'Nope, I reckon it don't.'

'Those gun-marks on his hands, they don't mean anything. You've got them. So have Bix Smith and Simon Girty.'

Braden chuckled. 'Pull your horns in, gal. I'm not allowing that Pinkertons or the law's after him. It's just a mite unusual for a man to come in off the range wounded like that and without any duffle along of him.'

'He could have come from Two Forks.'

'The way he come in?' Braden scoffed. 'He didn't ride far with that wound.'

'We'd best leave it until dawn before you start in to wiring the Pinkertons and telling them we've caught Butch Cassidy, or Sam Bass.'

'I ain't going to argue with you, gal. You're a whole lot like your mammy in that.'

She looked at her foreman for a long moment, then asked, 'Why did you say that, Seth. You rarely mention my mother. What was she like? I can't remember anything about her.'

'Good, kind, square and a real lady,' replied Braden, slowly, as if feeling out each word before he said it. 'A man'd be proud to know her.'

'I wish I'd known her,' she sighed. 'Uncle Frank and Aunt Annie were always good and kind to me, so are you. But I wish I'd known my mother.'

At that moment Waco groaned and the girl turned her attention to him. Braden looked relieved as if he did not wish to discuss the subject of Beth's mother with her. It was getting too hot for comfort and Braden took his chance to join the other men of the crew, leaving Beth to tend to the stranger who had come in out of the night.

Beth bedded the wounded young man down as comfortably as she could, then rolled into her blankets near to him. The girl got little sleep that night; she would doze off, then wake to look at the still form beside the fire.

The following morning at dawn, Beth rolled from her blankets. She went to Waco and looked down at him. His eyes were open and she thought she'd never seen such nice, blue eyes.

'Howdy,' she said gently. 'How do you feel?'

Slowly Waco forced himself into a sitting position. He looked up at the most beautiful face he'd ever seen. Not even the marks of the fight made Beth any less beautiful to the young Texan. His hand went up to touch the bandage around his head and he winced.

'What happened? Where am I?'

Gently the girl moved his hand from the bandage and ordered, 'You lay still a minute. You'll be all right. That was a real nasty graze you collected. How did it happen?'

A puzzled look came to Waco's face. He shook his head as if trying to clear it, then felt the bandage again.

'I don't know, ma'am. I surely don't know. Who am I?'

'Who are you?' Beth felt silly repeating the words, but she could not prevent herself from doing so. 'Don't you know who you are?'

'I can't remember,' there was worry in Waco's voice. He started to force himself up. 'I don't know——'

'Easy now, easy,' she replied, easing him down again. 'You're wearing Texas clothing and the big paint horse belongs to you. Does that help?'

'No, ma'am.'

The girl looked at the horse, it was grazing near the camp and as it turned she could see the brand it carried. She licked her lips which suddenly felt dry and tried to help him.

'The horse is branded CA, that's a ranch owned by a man called Clay Allison. You talk like a Texan.'

'Could be, ma'am,' he answered. 'But I surely wouldn't know about it.'

The girl straightened up, her face working sadly. She wondered if the close-passing bullet could cause the man to lose his memory. She knew instinctively that he was not lying to her. She'd been well educated and knew that loss of memory could result from a blow on the head, and, even though it merely grazed the side of the head, the bullet must have struck hard. The Texan talked rationally, yet he was clearly puzzled.

'Well, until you can remember, I'll call you Texas,' she said. 'I've got to talk with my foreman. You lay there for a spell, then I'll bring you some food.'

Braden saw the girl's face as she came towards him. He knew there was something badly wrong but was not prepared for what she told him in reply to his:

'Who is he?'

'He doesn't remember who he is, or anything about himself.'

'Yeah?' grunted Braden sceptically.

'He doesn't!' snapped Beth, stamping her foot. 'It's true. I know it is. He wouldn't lie to me.'

Braden started to say something, saw the glint in her eyes and knew better. He grinned wryly and squeezed her arm, then said, 'You're all right, girl. And you surely wouldn't hurt a living thing.'

Beth managed to smile back, for she was very worried and disturbed by the presence of that handsome young man.

'I surely tried to hurt that girl yesterday. I'll take him his breakfast over. He'll have to come with us, and stay until he remembers who he is.'

Braden watched her go, watched the way she sat and talked with the stranger. There was a grim look on his face as he looked at the young Texan who was now sitting by Beth and eating a hearty breakfast.

'That gal thinks she loves you, stranger,' Braden hissed under his breath. 'You hurt that gal and I'll kill you.'

CHAPTER NINE

TEXAS PROVES HIS WORTH

'AIN'T love wonderful?' Darkie White inquired of his friends.

The rest of the BM hands greeted the remark with knowing grins and wise nods as they studied their boss-lady and the tall young Texan who sat next to her on the wagon-box.

'Seth,' the girl remarked casually, 'I think Darkie had best ride the East line for a spell.'

Braden nodded in agreement while Darkie howled his protests to the skies. The East line was one of the dark cowhand's pet hates. It was boggy land and the line rider spent much of his time hauling cattle out of the mud. Darkie tended to be something of a dandy dresser and hated getting his clothes all muddied up.

'Serves you right,' the hand called Johnny said severely. 'Putting your big ole nose into other folks' love-lives.'

'And there's a whole lot of fence digging on the spread that'll just be Johnny's big enough,' Beth went on cheerily.

That ended the comments. Beth knew how to handle her crew, knew all their likes and dislikes. When they riled her she could always find some task they particularly disliked to give them.

Braden was worried as he watched the girl. She hated to ride on the wagon, but this day insisted that she did so, sitting next to the stranger who she'd also decided was unable to ride his horse.

The girl talked with Waco, trying to help him discover who he was. He knew about the range and the cattle, but it was his past life, his name and other personal details he did not remember. She was more than sure he really knew nothing and that he was not trying to trick her. She was puzzled by this and thought of what they knew. His horse was good, better than the usual run of cowhorses. His saddle was a plain, very well-used cattle rig and his rope was more than a decoration. He'd worn a gunbelt and two guns, that was far from usual; the men who wore two guns, were either trying to bluff people into thinking they were tough, salty and good—or they were tough, salty and good. That rifle was not a cowhand's weapon either, although there was no reason why a cowhand should not own one if he wished. His lack of a bedroll was another unusual thing. She wondered if she should send word to Two Forks and have that Drifter Smith, the sheriff, come out to take a look.

Behind the wagon the rest of the hands were just as interested in Waco.

'Wonder who he are?' asked Darkie White.

'Been a cowhand,' Braden replied. 'Least, his hands carry the marks.'

'Used him a gun more than a might,' Angus McKie remarked.

'Any man who rides the range's likely to,' Braden growled. 'I've never seen none of you bunch riding around naked.'

'Ain't every man who shows that he's been toting a brace,' Angus stated. 'I never seen many who wore two and less that looked as if they could handle both of 'em when they did. He can. Look at that rifle of his'n.'

Not knowing the interest he was causing, Waco relaxed, listening to the talk of the pretty girl by his side. He could never remember when he knew another girl like this one, for the voice raised stirrings in his heart. His mind was working, trying to probe back and remember who he was, what he was doing here.

At last the girl pointed ahead to her home. 'That's our place, Texas.'

Waco looked ahead. Near a small clump of scrub-oaks, with a stream running in a curve around it, lay the BM ranch-house. It was a small, neat two-storey stone building, fresh painted and pleasant looking. The bunkhouse lay off to the left, a few smaller buildings behind it and the usual three corrals out front. All in all it looked like a middle-sized, well-cared-for ranch, the sort of place Waco would have dreamed of owning, had he ever found time for dreaming.

'Nice spread you've got there, ma'am,' he said.

Beth eyed him with mock severity. 'I'm not going to tell you the name's Beth any more.'

Three men came from the bunkhouse, making for the corral to greet the rest of the ranch crew. The hands attended to their horses, telling of their adventures in town and describing the fight to the other two old BM hands. The third man was mostly ignored. He was a tall, handsome man with black hair and a close-trimmed moustache. His dress was good, a rangeland dandy with a low hanging Colt gun in his holster. There was arrogance in his every line as he studied Waco, watching the Texan turning his paint into an empty corral.

'Who's this?' he asked, glancing at the bandage around Waco's head.

'A new hand. His name's Texas,' replied Beth, not hiding her dislike of the handsome man.

'Looks like a bagline bum to me,' grunted the cowhand. 'I didn't know you wanted any new hands.'

'I hire, or fire, who I please,' Beth snapped. 'You remember that, Jack Hatch. Did you dig that new backhouse hole?'

'Got started on it, but we was too busy guarding the spread.'

'You'll push your luck just too far, Hatch,' barked Braden. 'I'm getting sick of you and your ways.'

'Yeah?' Hatch grinned, hand lifting over the butt of his gun.

'Seth!' Beth spoke quickly, trying to prevent trouble. 'Take Texas to the bunkhouse and see he gets bedded in. Windy, tote Texas's kak up to the barn and put it on the burro for him.'

Waco drew the rifle from the saddleboot and followed Braden towards the bunkhouse. The rest of the hands followed along, talking among themselves, while one of the pair who'd stayed on at the ranch picked up Waco's saddle and toted it to the barn.

Hatch watched the others go and there was dark anger on his face as he followed them. Beth watched him and went along to the house where a fat old Osage woman stood waiting on the porch. She was Little Doe, Beth's housekeeper, maid and one-time nurse. The girl went to the old Indian woman and began telling her about the man who had come so sud-

86

denly into her life.

Waco followed Braden into the large bunkhouse. He laid his rifle on the table in the room centre and went to the empty bunk the foreman showed him. The other hands entered the room, talking eagerly about the fight, the hand who'd missed it cursing his luck. None of them noticed Hatch come in, but the man crossed the room and stood looking at Waco.

'Hey you,' Hatch said loudly, bringing an end to all the talk. 'We don't like you here.'

Waco turned, looked the man over, seeing he was primed for trouble. 'We don't—or you don't?'

'Me for one. I don't like Texans any time. I like them a damned sight less when they can't remember their names.'

'Mister,' replied Waco. 'What you don't like'd be like to fill the big ole Grand Canyon.'

Hatch started as if Waco had slapped him in the face. There was sudden anger in his eyes. 'Why you damned saddle-tramp——!' he began, and made a mistake.

His fist shot out, smashing into Waco's face. He staggered back, hit the wall and Hatch came at him, ripping a punch which jerked his head to one side. Waco was taken by surprise but his instincts came to his aid. He'd learnt fist-fighting from a man who was acknowledged as being one of the finest rough-house brawlers in the West. Mark Counter's lessons came in useful right now. Waco's left arm came up to deflect the next punch, his right ripped into Hatch's stomach, bringing a grunt of pain. Waco brought up his left, snapping Hatch's head back and before the dandy got a chance to recover, Waco drove across the right. The dandy staggered back across the room and went down. He came up again, his Colt falling from the holster, but did not get a chance. Waco attacked fast, his fists slamming the man across the room before him. Hatch hit back, spinning Waco on to a bunk. Then Hatch dived across the room, hand clawing for his gun.

That was when the ranch crew saw how fast Waco could move when needed. The young Texan went over the table in a rolling dive, scooping up the rifle as he went. He hit the floor and the rifle bellowed, the heavy bullet smashing the revolver from under Hatch's hand.

In the same move Waco rolled to one knee, the rifle lever

blurred and the muzzle lined on Hatch's chest.

'Freeze hard, you lousy rat,' he snapped.

The bunkhouse door was flung open hard enough to almost jar it from its hinges and Beth came in. She tried to get through the bunch of cowhands and her body felt suddenly cold as she heard Braden say:

'You lousy rat, Hatch. The boy wasn't wearing a gun.'

'Surely got hisself one fast enough though,' whooped Angus delightedly. 'And ole Jacky there's been telling us *he* was fast.'

Waco ignored all this, laying his rifle on the table and clenching his fists. 'You all wanting to carry on with it?'

Slowly Hatch came to his feet, rubbing the blood from his face and tried to meet the angry blue eyes. He knew that here was a master with fists or with any kind of weapon.

Before he could say anything, there came a violent interruption. Beth was in front of him, her eyes glowing with fury. The cowhands stared, they'd never seen the girl so angry.

'You get off this ranch right now, Jack Hatch!' she snapped, the combined fury and loathing in her voice making him take a pace back. 'You dirty bully, attacking a sick man.'

Darkie gave a whooping laugh. 'Ole Texas hits that way sick, I'm not fixing to tangle with him when he's well again.'

'Darkie boy,' agreed Johnny. 'You're right for the first time in your young and wuthless life.'

Hatch looked around, seeing the derision and dislike on every face. His eyes went to the tall young Texan and he snarled, 'The next time we meet I'm shooting.'

'You just now tried,' replied Waco grimly. 'Why wait until next time?'

'Let up, Texas,' growled Braden. 'You got half an hour to get off this place, Hatch. See you've gone.'

Beth looked at the tall Texan and asked how he was. There were grins from members of the ranch crew at the girl's concern, but none of them made a comment about it. The tension was still in the air and stayed until Hatch gathered his gear and left, heading for the corral.

Waco remained ready for trouble until the other man left, then he relaxed and was ready to become friendly with the others. Darkie White stepped up, watching the door close behind Beth, for the girl rarely came into the bunkhouse. That was the home of the cowhands and not a place for a woman.

'Texas, come and get acquainted with this 'ere bunch. Ain't one of them wuth a cuss dead or alive, but you'll have to put up with 'em.'

'Sure, but I'm lucky.'

'Why?' asked Darkie.

'I've only got to put up with them, they've got to put up with me—and you.'

So Waco took on yet another name; he became Texas to the crew. In the days which followed, while Bix Smith tried and failed to follow his tracks, Waco stayed on at the BM house. He quickly became very popular with the others and was Beth's favourite, although he never played on it, nor, after the first day, received any special treatment.

His wound was not serious or troublesome and he was the first out to work every morning. He proved that he was a cowhand of the first water and could handle any horse in the remuda, although Beth would have strenuously objected had she known.

Braden watched the tall young man, wondering about him. That he was a tophand went without saying. Braden was willing to concede that Waco was as skilled with cattle as the foreman himself. They'd seen how he could use that rifle and handle his fists. They'd also seen how fast he could act when it was called for. Yet, for a man who showed signs of wearing two guns, he showed little skill when he borrowed a gunbelt and tried fast draw and shoot. That was easily explained. The cowhands did not wear double holstered belts, nor were their holsters worked on to give that extra ease of grip which a fast gunman needed. There was another thing, although Braden could not know this, that Waco's matched guns were of the five-and-a-half-inch-barrelled Artillery Peacemaker model. The ranch crew all owned Colt Peacemakers, but of the more usual seven-and-a-half-inch Cavalry or four-and-three-quarter-inch Civilian model. So the guns Waco was loaned did not balance in his hands; he could hit his mark, but not with the speed or accuracy he could attain with his own guns.

Five days passed. Waco settled down to his new life and worked hard. He was at the house for dinner most nights and was often seen taking walks with Beth in the moonlight. There were significant glances among the other men at this for the young Texan was a true cowhand and averse to walking any more than was necessary.

All in all, the hands approved of Waco as being nearly worthy of their boss-lady. Angus said a word about it as they gathered by the corral ready to go out to work some cattle after lunch on the fifth day.

'I like Texas,' he said profoundly. 'He stands full seventeen hands high and he's making a hand. But he's got to prove he's worth it afore he marries our gal.'

'Plays him a mean hand of poker,' Johnny remarked casually.

Angus grunted. He was the authority on the noble art of filling the inside straight but in Waco met his match. It was a friendly game and Angus tried to make an alteration in the run of the cards by holding out a couple of aces ready for use. He got his chance to use them on Waco's next deal, when, after an apparently harmless riffle, and the deck being cut, Waco dealt Angus a pair of aces. These, with his held-out pair, gave Angus a hand which might be expected to clean out the board. It was a good thought but failed, due to Waco producing a small straight flush. The young Texan then proceeded to show the others a whole lot about crooked gambling that they'd never seen nor heard of before.

'He can handle his ole paint hoss as well,' said Angus snuffily.

Johnny grinned wryly, his hand going to the battered old hat he wore. On the morning after their return from town he tried to take a short cut through the corral which housed Waco's paint and found the huge stallion charging at him. To escape, Johnny threw his hat into the horse's face and lit out for the corral rails. His hat was stamped to dollrags but he was fairly philosophical about it. The hat was brand new but all he said was :

'Could have been wuss. My head might have been in it.'

Braden settled back, listening to the comments. He glanced at Darkie who wore a new shirt, having been forced to scrub all his other clothes after riding the East line in an unusually hard patch of cattle getting into the mud. The dark cowhand saw Waco and Beth approaching so began to whistle the

Wedding March.

Beth listened for a moment, there was a mild expression on her face and she cooed like a dove as she remarked, 'Isn't it about Darkie's turn to ride the East line again, Seth?'

Darkie raised his hands. 'I'll be good,' he promised. 'You just go and pick on one of the others for a change.'

'I'll surely do that,' she promised, eyeing the grinning cowhands grimly. 'Especially if I find out who put the stinkweed outside my door and left a nice lil note fastened to it.'

'Note?' asked the culprit, Johnny. 'War there a note—and some stinkweed?'

'There was,' said Beth grimly. 'And it wasn't Angus, he can't write. Darkie always spells love with a "u", two "v's" and no "e". I saw a letter he wrote to Dolly Weller in town once.'

Waco knew who'd left the bunch of stinkweed, with the charming little note reading, *From Texas with luv.*' He did not say anything, but that night, when Johnny jumped into bed, he found it filled with the foul-smelling weed.

'Hoss coming in fast,' Darkie said, before Beth could continue trying to discover who left the stinkweed. 'Looks like Windy, but he don't ride that fast less'n there's food at the end of it.'

The girl turned and looked to where a rider was riding towards the ranch house. She recognised the approaching man but did not speak. The cowhand came up fast, bringing his horse sliding to a halt before the ranch foreman.

'Seth, they've been slow-elking.'

'How many?' growled Braden grimly. Slow-elking was killing stock, butchering some other man's cattle, and treated in the same way as rustling.

'I found six.'

'Six head?' Beth snapped angrily. She did not mind a passing stranger killing one steer if driven to it by hunger, but this was wholesale butchery. 'Get your horses, Seth, Texas, Darkie, Angus, Johnny. Windy, take another horse from your string and come with us.'

The men did not wait to talk about things. They darted for the corral and caught their horses while the other hands headed for the bunkhouse to collect weapons and ammunition for the party. One came up with Waco's rifle and the box of bullets, handing it to the Texan.

'You want to borrow my Colt, Texas?' he asked.

'Reckon I'd best stick to what I know,' replied Waco.

The party rode from the ranch. The girl sat her little dun, a grim look on her face. There was no joking among the hands either, they rode in silence. This butchering was a grim business and not one of them felt like joking.

Windy led the others at a fast lope across the range and brought his horse to a halt, pointing ahead.

'Down there in them bushes. Saw some buzzards, dropping towards something and come over to take a look. Was a piece of gut they'd thrown out.'

Beth started her horse forward but Waco stopped her. His instincts were now those of a lawman. 'Hold hard, boss-lady,' he said. 'Suppose we all stops here and just gets down first.'

'What do you mean?' she asked.

'Could likely cut for sign afore this heavy-footed bunch tramples everything flat into the ground.'

The girl saw the sense in Waco's suggestion. If there was sign they might be able to read it and discover where the men who did the butchering went. There was only one snag which met her eyes.

'All right. But none of us are much good at reading sign. Nothing to make old Tom Horn worried, anyways.'

'I'll make a try,' Braden growled, 'although I'm not good. Sure wish we'd got Lil Doe's brother along, he could read sign.'

'How about you giving her a whirl, Texas?' asked Darkie mildly. 'You read any sign?'

'Just about follow a dragged log through sand,' Waco replied, something swirling through his head, some vague memory. It was gone before he could grasp it but he knew he could read sign. 'If it's soft sand that is.'

Braden and the girl exchanged glances. They'd wondered about the things Waco remembered, trying to fix together a picture of him as he was before the shooting. He knew much about guns and about the skills of the crooked gambler, although they doubted if he was the latter. Now he appeared to know something about tracking.

Beth frowned, the Texas man showed many of the talents of

a town-taming lawman. Strangely, she never thought to connect this tall, handsome young Texan with her imaginary
picture of the stern, thirty-year-old or more, lawman for whom
she voted in the elections. She never connected her Texas with
Drifter Smith, sheriff of Two Forks county.

CHAPTER TEN

TEXAS READS SIGN

WACO moved forward, studying the intestine laying on the ground. The buzzards had been at it but there was enough left for him to find it with no difficulty. Then he saw something more, something which brought him to a halt. Slightly away from the length of intestine were the tracks of one man, leading down into a small bushy hollow, where the actual butchering was done, out of sight of any chance passing cowhand.

The tracks came out and returned and from all the signs the man had carried the piece of intestine out with him, to leave it on the ground. Waco was puzzled by this action. Why would a man take the trouble to carry a piece of offal out of the bushes after taking so much trouble to hide while doing the butchering? It just did not make any sense at all.

Following the tracks Waco was even more puzzled. The man was not tall, the length of the stride showed that. He was wearing moccasins not cowhand boots, but he was no Indian, he toed out in a way no Indian did when walking. Besides, no Indian would bother to butcher cattle. He would take the horns, hide, meat, bone, tallow and bellow but he would take them alive, on the hoof and save carrying.

The rest of the BM crew watched as Waco went forward, disappearing into the bushes. He found where the steers were butchered with no trouble. In the centre of the bushes was an open space and there was plenty of sign which showed the butchering was done there.

Waco went over the ground, noting that all the horses ridden by the butchers were shod, something no Indian pony ever was. He saw six different patches of blood where the cattle were killed. From the way the blood was dried, the horse droppings and other sign, he could guess how long the operation took. The men who killed the cattle were experts, that was plain from the speed they worked at. The bones and offal were cleaned down from the useful meat.

It was then Waco noticed the hides were missing. He prowled through the bushes trying to find where the skins were buried, but could not and was forced to assume the butchers took the hides with them.

Returning to the open ground he saw something on the ground, a small black object. Bending down he picked the thing up, rolling it in his fingers and examining it, before slipping it into his pocket. He searched on, picking up four more of those small black objects and pocketing them. Then he walked back out of the bushes to where the others were waiting more or less patiently for him.

'Go ahead,' he said. 'There's not a lot to see.'

'It took you long enough to see it,' replied Beth. 'May we be allowed to ask what you found?'

'Sure, go ahead,' said Waco, and mounted his paint.

Almost a minute ticked by while Beth glared at the imperturbable Texan. She looked ready to explode as she yelled:

'Dangnab it if you're not getting as bad as the rest of the bunch. All right! All right! What did you find?'

'You really want to know?'

Beth's face turned red and she told Waco in hide-searing terms just what she thought of him, his findings, the State of Texas, the Confederate States, then wound up with a demand to know all he found out, before she pulled off his arm and beat his fool head in with it.

'Was four of them,' Waco drawled. 'Three tallish, one shorter. Short *hombre* with a tooth missing out the front of his mouth, smokes ceegars most all the time and wears moccasins. I'd allow he was a skin-hunter. Ever run across anybody like him afore, Seth?'

Braden shook his head, grinning at the surprised looks on the faces of the others. Here was a sign reading that took some beating, if Texas was right.

'Didn't you ask him his name?' Darkie inquired. 'You knowing this here short-growed ceegar-smoker so well.'

'How do you know so much about the small man, Texas?'

inquired Beth.

'That's what Darkie meant, but he's too polite to up and ask.'

Silence came again but Beth's breathing rose to a pitch. 'Seth,' she finally said, 'I reckon it's time we got this uppy Johnny Reb on the blister-end of a shovel for a spell.'

Waco decided that this was a time when discretion would be the better part of valour. Beth meant what she said and he never took kindly to digging.

'He smoked these five cigars while they were doing the skinning,' he explained, showing the stubs. 'Like I said there were four men, all skin-hunters from the boots they wore. Four of them wouldn't take so all-fired long to butcher and dress out six head of cattle. Means he must have darned nigh lit one cigar as soon as he finished the other. Could tell about the missing tooth from the marks on the stubs. The small man was the one doing the smoking. I could tell that from his sign. He was the one who carried that lump of gut out here. What I want to know is why and we'll likely find that out at the end of the tracks when they pulled out. Reckon we ought to follow them, boss-lady?'

'How'd you mean, you don't know why he carried the lump of gut out with him, Texas?' Beth asked.

'How'd you happen to come across the butchering, Windy?' said Waco, not answering the girl's question directly.

'Saw buzzards rising and come over this way to see what was happening.'

'Sure, you saw buzzards dropping,' Waco agreed.

'That was to the lump of gut that lay out there,' Darkie interrupted with a grin. 'Or was you looking so hard at that short *hombre* that you never saw it?'

'I saw it, saw that the short *hombre* toted it out there,' replied Waco, eyeing Darkie as if he was something fresh crawled from under a rotten log. 'So why'd they bother to hide in the bushes there?'

'Thought even a Texan'd be able to figger that out,' Angus scoffed. 'So they wouldn't get seen. It'd likely be months afore any of us went into them bushes and found they'd been at butchering our stock. If we ever did.'

'That's smart figgering, real smart. They must have been

96

Scotch,' drawled Waco, ignoring Angus's comment that the term was Scot, not Scotch. 'They goes to all that trouble to hide away some place that nobody'll find what they been doing. Then they totes a lump of gut out to bring down buzzards.'

With that he started his horse forward, circling the clump of bushes. The others followed him, clearly all thinking about the peculiar circumstance of the piece of gut. They would probably never have given it a thought had Waco not mentioned it to them.

The slow-elking party had made no great attempt at hiding their sign. Even so, with the short grass and everything, it would take a man who knew how to read sign to follow the tracks. Waco rode easily, his eyes on the way the grass was crushed down, the tips pointing in the direction the men travelled. He looked ahead at the broken country which they were approaching and brought his horse to a halt.

'Boss-lady,' he said, reaching down and drawing the rifle from his saddleboot. 'You'd best head back for the spread, or get back to the rear of the bunch and stay there.'

'Why' she asked, bristling at his words.

'They might be laying for us.'

Braden swore under his breath. He'd not thought of the men they were following waiting for them in ambush. The girl, riding at the forefront of the party, would have formed the first target. She looked first at Braden, then at Waco, and without another word went to the back of the party.

They followed the sign for about a mile, going slowly and with every member of the BM party alert for trouble. Then Waco stopped his horse, looking down at the tracks with more care than he'd shown before. He swung from his horse to bend over and examine the surrounding area.

'Tracks go on that ways,' Darkie said impatiently. 'Headed towards the Mormon country.'

Waco looked as if he was going to make some reply. Then he stopped, swung afork his big paint, winked at Braden to prevent the foreman saying anything and rode forward. He turned in his saddle and warned the others to keep their fool horses set off the tracks as much as they could and rode on. He could see nearly every part of this business now and knew that it could become deadly dangerous if things went wrong.

'Hold it!' he hissed, bringing the others to a halt. 'Keep the hosses here. Darkie, get them out of sight. The rest of you come with me.'

The men obeyed Waco without a thought as to his right to give them the orders. They dismounted, allowing Darkie to lead their horses away and followed Waco as he darted forward following the line of tracks. Faintly they heard the sound of approaching horses and Waco waved to the sides of the tracks. The party split up, half going to either side and taking cover.

Beth slid down behind the rock where Waco was kneeling, holding his rifle. She watched his face, seeing how old, hard and strong it looked. It was no longer the face of a friendly cowhand, but of a grim, masterful and determined man. She held down her interested and excited questions for the sound of hooves were coming nearer all the time.

A dirty-looking Indian wearing cast-off white man's clothing and nursing a Springfield '73 carbine that looked as if it might have been taken from one of Custer's men after the Little Big Horn battle, came into view. Behind him came half a dozen soberly dressed, well armed Mormons, riding slowly but with some caution. They appeared to be following the same tracks as Beth's party, but were headed in the opposite direction.

'Hold it up, gents!' called Waco as the men came alongside the ambush position taken by the cowhands. 'We've got you surrounded.'

The Mormons brought their horses to a stop, hands dropping towards their hips but freezing as they saw that Waco told the simple truth. The bearded man who rode at the head of the party asked:

'Who be ye?'

'We'll do the asking, seeing' how we got our guns lined,' replied Waco. 'I tell you, we ride for the BM. Light down and talk this out with us.'

The Mormon made no attempt to accept Waco's offer. They remained on their horses, with their hands resting on their guns. Their leader looked at Waco as the young Texan stepped from behind the rock, followed by the girl.

'What do you here. This is close to being our land.'

'Likely,' agreed Waco. 'But these rifles make us tellers, not askers. Climb down and talk, it'll be easier on us all.'

The Mormon leader looked first at Waco, who lowered his rifle, then at the girl as she came to join him. There was no treachery planned, the girl showed that the Gentile cowhand was willing to talk. He would never have risked letting her come out if shooting was planned.

'We will talk,' he said and dismounted.

'Put the guns down, boys,' called Waco. 'Now, friend. You tell me all about how you found cattle butchered, the hides gone and started to trail the men who did it.'

The Mormon shrugged. 'You appear to know as much about it as I do.'

'Why're you following these tracks?' Beth snapped angrily. 'They lead to——'

'They don't, boss-lady,' Waco interrupted. 'This lot're pointing back the way we come, right to where I stopped and that great expert at reading sign, Mr. Darkie White took over the sign-reading for us.'

'Texas's right, Beth gal,' Braden grunted. 'I saw it but he wigwagged me not to say anything.'

'Sure, our set finished and this bunch carried on, so I just kept quiet 'n' watchful, back-lining this lot. Didn't know if we'd meet you gents, but I was on the look out.'

'How did you know that hides were missing?' asked the Mormon.

'They took our'n. So I figgered they'd have your'n, too. Why'd a man who's been slow-elking take the hides with him?'

'Steer hides bring in money,' Beth pointed out, pleased that she'd found a thing Texas did not think of. 'And they wouldn't want the hides to be found——'

'Sure, they wouldn't want the hides found. So they tote along the only one thing that'd prove they'd butchered your stock,' finished Waco, even as the girl saw what he was getting at.

'All but one of our hides was taken,' remarked the Mormon.

'And that one didn't carry a brand,' guessed Waco.

His guess was a meat-in-the-pot hit. That showed from the expression which flickered briefly across the Mormon's face:

'How do you know?' he asked.

'Only reason they'd leave the hide behind. A green hide's not light, they wouldn't want to tote weight along that wasn't necessary.'

'These are strange doings, Gentile,' said the Mormon thoughtfully. 'How do you explain them?'

'Figger that tonight there's going to be some moving, or real soon. Your hides are brought and hid on the BM place and our'n turn up on your land. What I want for you——' Waco stopped speaking and turned to the girl. 'I'm sorry, boss-lady. It's not for me to give orders.'

'It surely isn't,' she replied, smiling. 'But don't let that stop you *now*. I'll copper any bets you want to make.'

'Thank you 'most to death, ma'am,' drawled Waco, and she poked her tongue out at him. 'I want you to send two of your men to the BM with us, friend. And I want two of your boys to go to the Mormon place, boss-lady. Way I see it them skins'll be hid close to the house both times, so there's no chance them being missed by the law when they come.'

'You are a man of intelligence, Gentile,' said the Mormon. 'There are many of your people, and of mine, who would have started to shoot as soon as they met.'

'Somebody figgered on that, too. They allowed you and us'd likely all be following the sign, would meet up and start throwing lead. Which same's why they left the gut laying out there in the open, boss-lady. They wanted men to find the cattle and fast. Hoped that we'd meet up with these folks coming to look for their'n and start to throwing lead.'

'Who'd want that?' Beth asked without thinking. She could have bitten her tongue off as soon as she said the words.

'Boss-lady, I'm real wonderful, but I ain't got to where I can work miracles just yet. How'd I know who'd be behind it?'

Beth made a mental note that it was time Texas did some digging to teach him proper respect for a lady.

'What now?' she asked.

'We've been following the wrong set of tracks—now I aims to get on the right set and follow them to the end.'

Beth looked hard at Waco, listening to his soft drawled words. She knew just what he meant and did not like the sound of it. There were at least eight men involved in the butchering, she guessed. If the ranch crew got on the trail and found the men there was going to be shooting, killing, and she did not want that.

'All right,' she said grimly, eyeing the cowhands. 'Fun's over. If you'll tell off two of your men, Elder, we can head back for the BM.'

'How about me, boss-lady?' Waco asked mildly.

'Well, you can do as you like. But you don't go after that bunch alone and none of the boys are going, or the Mormons. You'd need some help to get those eight men and you're not getting it.'

'Sure I need help. I'd need about two troops of worthless Yankee cavalry to help. But I wasn't fixing to paint for war yet. I just want to find out where those slow-elkers are at,' drawled Waco, then turned to the Mormon. 'Can I use your Injun and take one of your men along with me to show them where——'

'Take Joshua, he's a good Indian. I would take your word for anything you find. Unless you want a man along also.'

'Less of us the better. I'd admire to have the Injun to help read sign. It won't be easy from where the two bunches met up.'

'I'm going with you, Texas,' said Beth in her most determined tone.

Waco gave in. He'd not known Beth long but he knew that tone. When it came a twenty mule team would not budge Beth Morrow from her decision. He whistled and his paint came to him, Darkie followed, bringing the other horses with him. The young Texan mounted and waited until the girl told Darkie and Angus to go with the Mormons.

The two parties separated and at the place where the two sets of tracks came together, Waco and the Indian stopped. Beth gave her orders to Braden, who left unwillingly. He knew the girl was in good hands, but wanted to get at the bottom of this mystery.

Waco and the Indian dismounted, they examined the grass with care and then both mounted. They separated and started to ride in a circle, using the place where Beth sat her horse as an axis. The first circle was about a hundred yards in diameter. They met, shook their heads, then made a second circle fifty yards larger. The young Texan halted his horse, removing his hat and waved it. The Indian and Beth converged on him and he indicated tracks of a large body of men.

'Old blanket trick,' Waco explained, in answer to Beth's question. 'Spread down blankets, move the hosses on to them. Lay three more in line, hoss gets to the end, you move the first one up and spread it. The blanket spreads the weight of the horse and doesn't leave no sign. It's slow, but it works.'

'But why did they do that——!' began Beth.

'Ugh! Plenty talking squaw you got there, white brother,' grunted the Indian. 'You not beat her enough.'

Beth chuckled but Waco's face flushed red. It was the first time in his life he had ever blushed and could not think of a reply. He started the horse forward along the tracks as Beth saw the young man's face.

They followed the sign on, leaving Beth's ranch and heading across country. The girl frowned, she knew where they were heading. They saw no sign of human life on the ride and there were few cattle even though this was good grazing land.

'We're making for Mr. Von Schnabel's ranch,' she said.

'He may be in on it then,' replied Waco. He was puzzled, the name meant something to him. He was sure of that, but could not say where or when he'd heard it before.

Beth nodded. She could see that Von Schnabel might profit from trouble with her ranch. The German had made her a good offer for her place, but she refused it and the subject was never mentioned again.

'The house is at the foot of that slope,' she went on.

They left their horses. The girl took a pair of powerful field-glasses from her saddle-pouch and joined the two men as they advanced on foot up the slope. They flattened at the top of the slope and looked down at the Von Schnabel ranch house. It was much the same in appearance as the BM, the layout roughly the same, the house and the bunkhouse separate buildings. Several men lounged around by the corral and the girl focused her glasses on them. She gave her full attention to a bunch of men who were obviously not cowhands. One caught her eye and she felt a thrill run through her. He was a smallish man, wearing buckskins and moccasins. A black cigar was between his teeth, a mere stub and even as she watched he took it from his mouth. The gap between his teeth showed plainly as he laughed at some comment made by one of the other men. He extracted another cigar, lit it from the stub and smoked on.

'The small man with the missing tooth,' she whispered and gave Waco the glasses. 'You wait until I tell Darkie and the others.'

Waco studied the ranch with some care. He examined the men, seeing that they were mostly gunhands or skinhunters. He also saw the five men he'd caught on the attempted stage hold-up, but they meant nothing to him.

Nodding to the others, Waco backed off. The Indian looked at him as they returned to the horses. 'Tell the Mormons, red brother,' he said. 'We'll go into town tomorrow and tell the law.'

Waco and the girl left the Indian and rode across country, making for the BM ranch. It was coming on dark and the girl rode near his side. She brushed against him, her hand reaching for his. His arm went around her and lifted her to his saddle. Their heads came close together, their lips meeting in a long kiss. Then he shook his head.

'This's no good, boss-lady. You don't know who I am, where I'm from, or any lil ole thing about me. I might be a ——'

'You're the man I love,' she replied. 'That's good enough for me.'

The two horses moved on side by side, the girl in Waco's arms. They talked as they rode, but the subject of steer butchering was never mentioned.

The following morning Beth, Waco and Johnny rode for town. During the night Waco's guess proved to be right. Three men rode up, leading a packhorse and carefully hid the Mormon steer hides in the woodpile at the back of the cook-shack. They moved well in the dark and it was almost a pity that Braden, Windy and the two Mormons watched their every move.

It was late afternoon as they rode across the cattle-bridge over the Colorado and along the deserted street. Waco was feeling uneasy, his memory fighting to break through the fogs as he looked at the town. There was no one in sight on the streets who might finally have helped jolt his memory. The livery-barn owner was absent, so they tended to their horses, taking their time with it.

'Best leave them in the corral,' said Beth, looking into the barn. 'All the stalls are taken.'

The horses went into the big, empty corral and then Beth turned. Her face suddenly lost all its colour.

Jack Hatch came walking around the corner of the livery-barn and she heard footsteps from the alley which lead from the street to the rear of the building.

'Texas!' Hatch yelled. 'Turn and fill your hand.'

Waco, unarmed, his rifle still in the boot on his saddle, turned to face the other man. Hatch grinned. Johnny wore a gun, but wasn't good with it, the girl wore a ·36 Navy Colt, rechambered for metallic cartridges, but she never showed if she could use it. This was the chance he'd wanted ever since the Texan beat him at the BM. With a grin which was pure hate Hatch dropped his hand, to bring his Colt from leather.

CHAPTER ELEVEN

SOME OF DRIFTER SMITH'S KIN

THEY came from the east. Four trail-dirty, unshaven young Texas men afork leg-weary horses, riding by the rear of the Twin Bridge Saloon.

Lynn Baker stood by the door and watched the four men ride by. What she saw worried her, for they were such men as she'd got to know among the fast guns of the Wild Bunch.

The first man was a giant, even in this land of tall men. Even afork his seventeen-hand blood-bay stallion his great height showed. He was a handsome, very handsome, man. Under his costly white JB Stetson, now dust covered and stained, showed curly golden blond hair. The face, even with the stubble of a few days, was almost classically handsome, but it was a tanned, strong face with no sign of weakness about it. A scarlet silk bandana was tight rolled around his throat, flowing long ends over the costly, made-to-measure tan shirt. His brown levis were also tailored to him and his boots were expensive. Around his waist was a brown buscadero gunbelt, a true fast man's rig, with matched ivory-handled Colt Cavalry Peacemakers in his holsters. He sat his plain Texas saddle with easy grace, a light rider for all his size. His bedroll and rope were slung from the saddle and a Winchester rifle's butt showed from under his left leg.

The second rider was astride as fine a looking horse as Lynn had ever known, a seventeen-hand white stallion. A huge, beautiful, yet somehow wild-looking creature, and the rider fitted such a mount. He was a tall, lithe-looking, black-dressed Texan. The stubble on his face appeared to make him look even younger than he was. His face was innocent-looking, dark and handsome, yet there was a look about him that was both wild and alien. His black clothes, from hat to boots, offered no change in colour. Around his waist was a black gunbelt; butt forward at the right was a walnut-handled old Dragoon Colt and an ivory-hilted bowie knife was sheathed at his left. From his saddleboot rose the hilt of an exceptionally fine Winchester.

The third rider was smaller than the others, not more than five foot six, she guessed. He was quietly dressed, inconspicuous, hardly noticeable in such company as he rode with. He was handsome enough, strong looking, with a black Texas style JB Stetson hat shoved back from a shock of dusty blond hair. His clothing was good, but somehow he did not show it off like the handsome giant, or the black-dressed boy. Not even the gunbelt, with the butt-forward, white-handled guns in the holsters, made him stand out any more. He rode a huge paint stallion not an inch smaller than the blood-bay or white. It was not the sort of horse one would expect so insignificant a man to be riding. Yet he sat his horse with that undefinable air which marked a tophand from the rest of the herd. From under his leg showed the butt of a Winchester carbine.

The last rider was tall, as tall as the black-dressed boy; slim, pallid and somehow studious looking, even with the stubble on his face. Yet there was a lithe power about him that did not go with such a face. He rode a big black horse, his clothing that of a working cowhand. His brown coat had the right side stitched back to leave clear the ivory butt of the Colt Civilian Peacemaker in the gunfighter's holster at his side.

'Where'd a man find the livery barn, ma'am?' asked the handsome giant, halting his horse and looking down at Lynn.

Lynn told him, studying them all. She'd seen hard men, fast men, in plenty, but here were four who could handle the best she'd seen. Even the small man, when she came to look more closely at him. They did not waste time in small talk, but turned their horses and rode off towards the barn.

The girl was worried as they went by. They were four real hard men and they were on the prod, or she missed her guess. If they were going to work for Von Schnabel there would be bad trouble. Even if Waco was in town he would have trouble in handling four men like those.

The owner of the livery barn studied the newcomers with some interest. At first he thought the paint belonged to Drifter

Smith. The small man was not such a fine figure as Drifter Smith though, even if he was a Texan. The owner of the barn saw the way each man set his guns right as soon as he dismounted. They did it instinctively, it was the mark of the real good man with a gun.

'We'll treat 'em to a stall each, friend,' the blond giant remarked as he dismounted.

On the ground his great size and the spread of his shoulders was emphasised by the way he towered over the other three.

'Sure thing, mister,' replied the owner. 'Four stalls?'

'One each, apiece,' agreed the dark-faced, innocent-looking rider of the white. There was something wild and Indian about him that showed to the old-timer's eyes. 'Happen you don't want none of your stock eating. This here Nigger hoss of mine's the only carnivorous hoss in the world.'

'Looks like it, too,' grunted the old-timer.

'You can hold our duffle until we find a place to stay,' said the small man, his eyes ranging around the horses in the stalls.

There were questions the old-timer would have liked to ask but his conversational attempts fell on stony ground and he got grunts in reply. He watched the four men tending to their horses with worried eyes. They were Texans and they'd rode far and fast. That showed in the signs. They were cowhands and good ones, that also showed, as did the fact that their guns were more than show-off decorations. They were too quiet, and silence in a cowhand was an ominous sign.

By the time the horses were attended to and the four men left, the owner of the barn knew one thing about them. The blond giant was called Mark, the black-dressed youngster was Lon, the small man Dusty and the other Doc. The names tied into something.

He walked to the door of the barn and looked out, watching the four Texans walking along the street. He scratched his stubby jaw and growled:

'Now who be ye? Them names tie into something. That small man though, naw, he cain't be. I'd say you was some of Drifter Smith's kin for all of that.'

'Make a start at the Guesthouse, that's where Frank said to look,' the small man called Dusty remarked as they halted on the street.

'Could see the jailhouse first,' the big man replied. 'See if the boy's come back.'

'Take the Guesthouse first, I didn't see any sign of his horse in the barn.'

The four men walked slowly along the street. They halted outside the Guesthouse, standing on the sidewalk and looking around them. Then they heard a woman scream in pain and thrust open the batwing doors. What they saw made them take sudden and violent action.

The bar-room was empty, all except for some dozen gun-hung men and four or five girls. All were looking at two men who held a pretty, red-haired girl over a table while a big, gambling man used a quirt on her already lacerated back.

'You lousy slut,' Matt Kyte, the quirt user, yelled. 'We caught you this time going to that bitch across the street. Tell us about——'

Mark thrust forward faster than any of the others. He caught up a heavy table and with a heave of powerful muscles sent it flying across the room as if it were made of paper. One of the men holding the girl gave a yell as the table hit him and knocked him staggering.

'What the hell?' Kyte snarled, turning.

Mark followed the chair up; he back-handed the other man from the girl, spinning him across the room and into the bar. Then, as Kyte swung up the quirt to strike at Mark, the Texan hit. It was a beautiful blow, thrown with the weight of the giant body behind it. Kyte's head snapped back, the quirt flew from his hand, he went backwards across the room, arms flailing and crashed into a table, smashing it under him.

The other men whirled ready to take cards in the game, but Ben Wharton, eyes bulging out in fear at the sight of the four men, gave a warning:

'Hold it. That's Dusty Fog, Mark Counter, the Ysabel Kid and Doc Leroy.'

The first three names were more than enough to halt the crowd, though the last one was not exactly unknown in its own right.

Dusty Fog, the quiet, insignificant-looking young man, the man who might be overlooked in peaceful times. The small man who'd been one of the Confederate Army's top three raiders, ranking with John Singleton Mosby and Turner Ashby, a captain at seventeen. The man who was segundo of the mighty OD Connected ranch in Texas, was known as trail boss, round-up captain, town-taming lawman. The Rio Hondo gun-wizard, the fastest of them all.

Mark Counter, the handsome blond giant who was even now moving in on Kyte. There was a man among men. His reputation as a fist fighter was without peer in the West. He was a tophand at the cattle business. There were many men who'd seen him in action that claimed he was almost as fast and accurate with his guns as his friend, Dusty Fog.

The third of the trio, the Ysabel Kid, was something of a name in his own right. They tell many tales on the United States-Mexican border of the black-dressed, baby-faced young man called the Ysabel Kid. Son of a wild Irish-Kentuckian father and a Creole-Comanche mother, the Kid was a dangerous young man. He was fast, if not exceptional, with his old Dragoon gun; with his knife he was acknowledged as being a real deadly dangerous fighting man, and with his rifle he was said to have no equal.

The fourth young man, that pallid, studious-looking cowhand, Doc Leroy, was not out of place in such a company. He made his name riding in the Wedge trail-crew herding cattle up the inter-state trails to the railheads in Kansas. Then he rode as a member of Ole Devil Hardin's floating outfit, the elite of the OD Connected ranch crew. Lately he'd been serving as an Arizona Ranger and had served with some distinction.

Kyte came up from the floor and charged at Mark Counter, to run into a man who really knew how to handle his fists. The gambler was not at his best from the first blow he took, and Mark beat him round the room. For all his size, Mark Counter was fast on his feet and his fists shot out like the stabbing tongue of a diamond-back rattler. Only they landed a whole lot harder, ripping into the gambler's face and driving him across the room.

A bouncer, full of misguided loyalty, caught Mark's arm to turn him. Mark came around fast. His right hand clamped on the bouncer's fat throat, the other hand gripped his waistband. Mark's muscles writhed and strained; the crowd let out a concerted gasp as fifteen stone of hard muscled flesh was lifted into the air and thrown over the bar.

Mark came around, sinking his fist almost wrist deep into Kyte's stomach, then ripped up a blow with the other hand. Kyte looked as if he was going in two directions at once. He crashed to his back and lay still. Mark scooped the gambler up, pulled his coat off, then ripped his shirt from his back and flung him face down on the table next to where the girl lay.

There was not a move in the place, except for Doc Leroy, who went to examine the girl's back. Mark stood for a moment, then went and picked up the quirt, holding it out to the nearest man.

'Use it on him!' Mark ordered. 'You being so all-fire keen on quirtings.'

'Like h——!' began the man.

Mark's fist, gripping the weighted butt of the quirt, drove up, the man's head snapped back and he crashed to the floor. Then Mark looked at Joe Brindle, the Cockney was trying to back away but got no chance.

'You make a start,' said Mark gently.

Brindle took the quirt and started to use it. He used it to such effect that Kyte was brought from consciousness by the pain and screamed as the lash bit him.

'Howdy, Bengeeman,' drawled the Kid, watching Wharton's face. 'Dusty, we done got ole Bengeeman here. Looks just as savage as when you run him outa Danby, Texas. Allow he ought to be the next to show us how she's done.'

Wharton gulped. He'd hoped that none of the trio would remember him from the skinner wars in Danby, Texas. They did remember. So did Wharton. He remembered a tall, good-looking youngster who rode with them. A blond-haired boy who rode a big paint stallion and handled a brace of matched Colts like a master. Then he remembered the name of Doc Leroy's Ranger partner and knew Drifter Smith's true identity. He gulped again. He'd killed Waco and now four friends of the young lawman were here and looking for the man who did it.

The whipping went on until every man in the place had taken his turn. Then Mark released the barely conscious, moaning gambler and stepped back.

'The girl walk, Doc?' he asked.

Doc Leroy shook his head, his eyes hard and cold as he looked at the hired gunmen. 'Nope. She's unconscious. Asked me to take her to the Twin Bridge Saloon.'

Mark stepped forward and lifted the girl gently, trying to avoid hurting her lacerated, bleeding back. He carried the girl from the saloon and the other three Texans started to back towards the door.

'We're not taking your guns,' remarked the Ysabel Kid. 'And we're surely hoping you try to use them.'

Which same was one hope the Kid would not get. Those gunmen knew that they were matched against three men who were well able to handle them. There was not a move made by any man in the room until the batwing doors swung closed on the Texans.

Mark was striding across the street, carrying the unconscious girl in his arms. The other three stood for a moment on the sidewalk, watching the saloon for some hostile sign but none came.

'Reckon they'll chance it, Dusty?' asked Doc.

'Not them,' replied Dusty with complete confidence. 'They don't want to take on nobody who knows how to handle guns.'

'This gal's hurt real bad, Dusty,' Mark called, waiting on the sidewalk outside the Twin Bridge Saloon. 'She's going to need a doctor.'

'We'll see she gets one—then we make a start at finding the boy.'

Ella Baker stared at the men as they came through the doors. Her eyes went to the form in Mark's powerful arms and she crossed the room. Lynn laid down the dice cup she'd been using in a friendly game of One Flop with the bartender, Madge, and followed her mother.

'What happened?' Ella asked, feeling suddenly cold, for she recognised the girl's red hair.

'Caught a bunch of guns quirting her across the street,' Mark replied. 'She needs doctoring, ma'am—and real fast.' Ella wasted no time in talk. She could see from the bloody mess on the girl's back that medical aid was needed. With that thought she turned and gave her orders to the watching girls:

'Lynn, go see if the doctor's fit to handle this. Madge, show

111

this gent to one of the rooms upstairs.'

Lynn started towards the door. Doc Leroy glanced at her, then looked again—hard. There was a look in his eyes which Dusty Fog never remembered seeing before and Doc said:

'That bunch from across the street might try and stop you, gal, I'd best go along with you.'

Dusty and the Kid eyed each other, grins coming to their lips as they watched the girl leave.

'Ole Doc went easy, *amigo*,' remarked Dusty.

Doc and the girl walked along the streets of the town. Lynn talked with him, freely and in a way which afterwards surprised her, for Lynn was a gal who knew something of men. She often wondered why she came to talk in such a manner to a complete stranger. They talked of many things, but strangely, the subject which brought Doc to Two Forks was not mentioned.

They reached the doctor's house without being molested by the men from the Guesthouse. Opening the door Lynn led the way into the reception room, a small, dusty and dirty looking place. For a time they stood waiting, then the girl went to a side door and listened at it. She turned the handle, opened the door and looked in. Doc Leroy stood behind her and what he saw brought an angry oath from his lips.

Stretched on the floor, an empty whisky bottle in his hand and his head in a pool of spilled Scalp-Lifter, lay the doctor, sole medical practitioner for two hundred miles.

Doc stepped forward, lifting the man's head and bending forward. The fumes of the cheap whisky hit him and his nose wrinkled in distaste. Pulling back the man's eyelid Doc looked at the pupil. He let the head drop back to the floor and came to his feet.

'Dead drunk,' he snapped. 'Won't be fit to work for a hell of a time.'

'He's often like that. Maw won't let him buy it in our place any more.'

Doc did not answer for a moment, his eyes going around the room. He made his decision. There was no time to worry over the morals of the situation, not with a girl's life at stake.

'Watch the street, gal,' he ordered. 'Tell me if you see anybody.'

The girl did as she was told. She heard the crash of breaking glass and turned to see Doc taking bottles and bandages from the doctor's glass-fronted supply cabinet. He took what he wanted, then made for the door.

'What're you fixing in to do, Doc?' Lynn asked, following him out on to the street.

'Looks like I'm going to need to do the chore myself.'

Ella was standing at the bar, talking with Dusty, Mark and the Kid when Lynn and Doc returned. She turned and looked at her daughter.

'Where's the doctor?'

'Stunk-up drunk as usual,' Lynn replied, then her face flushed and she went on. 'He's drunk again.'

'Now ma'am,' Doc put in, 'I'll want hot water, some clean white cloth, plenty of it. Get them sent up to wherever you've got the gal.'

'What do you mean?' she asked, looking at the pallid, studious face.

'Look ma'am,' Doc's voice took on a steely note. 'If something's not done for that gal, and done fast, you'll have a real dead friend.'

Ella's mouth dropped open, for once in her life she was unable to think of anything to say. Lynn took it out of her hands.

'You come with me, Doc,' she said. 'Madge, see that he gets all he wants.'

Madge grinned. 'You got a real grown-up daughter there, Ella,' she said and went to obey.

'What can he do?' Ella asked worriedly. 'It's work for a doctor.'

'Which same's just what Doc is, ma'am,' Dusty replied. 'He was within a year of finishing medical school when the Kiowas got his folks back home to Texas. Then his kid brother was killed in a stampede on the trail. He came back west and took on with the Wedge. I've seen him handle medical chores. He's the man who held the typhoid outbreak down to Canvastown last year.'

'There's three babies alive today who wouldn't have made it without Doc's help, ma'am,' Mark went on. 'I'd surely take it kind if I could wash up and shave.'

'Fetch your gear along and use my room,' Ella answered. 'Then I think we've got things to talk about.'

The Kid and Mark went to the livery-barn and brought back all four warbags to the Twin Bridge Saloon. They were all washed, shaved and changed; their dirty clothing taken to be washed by Ella, before Doc came from the other room. He grunted that the girl would be all right and they'd best keep a watch to make sure she did not get her face into the pillows. Then he went to wash, shave and change.

'You should have seen Doc work,' Lynn enthused as she came to join her mother and the Texas men. 'I've never seen a man with such gentle hands.'

'Why were that bunch cutting the gal up, ma'am?' Dusty asked. 'And why did she want to be brought across here?'

Ella did not reply to the question. She rose and crossed the room, returning with a staghorn-butted Colt Artillery Peacemaker in her hands. Dusty knew that gun, even without looking at the words inscribed on the backstrap.

> *To our pard, Waco from*
> *Ole Devil's Floating Outfit.'*

CHAPTER TWELVE

CAPTAIN FOG TAKES OVER

NONE of the three Texans spoke for a long moment as they looked at the Colt Ella Baker held towards them. They'd not introduced themselves but she knew who they were.

Dusty Fog broke the silence, his voice hard. 'Where'd you get that gun?'

Ella glanced around to make sure there was no one near enough to hear what she was going to say.

'The mate to this gun's down at the jail. I'll take you along to see Bix Smith and we'll tell you all we know.'

'Where's Waco?' growled Mark Counter.

'I don't know. Kate, the girl you brought in, she was trying to find out for certain what happened to him. They must have caught on to what she was doing for me.'

'And what *was* she doing for you, ma'am?' inquired Dusty.

'Finding out what the owner of the Guesthouse was up to. Kate's mother was German, she spoke the language fluently, although none of the bunch over there knew about it. She put me on to a few moves Von Schnabel was working on, then she went too far. She put the clocks back in the Guesthouse, even got into Von Schnabel's room and altered his watch while he was having a bath. That told them somebody was working against them. I should have got her out before——'

'Just what is this German trying to do, ma'am?'

'Take over everything in the town and county, Captain Fog. I believe he had the old sheriff killed and may have caused Waco's death, too.'

'The boy dead!' growled Mark Counter. 'Derry's telegraph message never said anything about that.'

'Derry?' asked Ella. 'You mean Frank Derringer?'

'Sure, ma'am,' agreed Dusty. 'We were in Arizona on business and called in at Terry Ortega's spread down to Backsight. Met up with Doc there and they told us how the boy'd come up here to avoid the Pinkertons. Then we got the telegraph message from Derry. He'd sent it to Terry Ortega, asking him to try and let us know that Waco was in trouble. We came straight up.'

'You allow it was one of that bunch from the Guesthouse?' said the Ysabel Kid mildly.

'I think it was Wharton.'

'Ole Bengeeman,' the Kid's words purred out like a cat playing with a mouse. 'It's a long time when me'n ole Bengeeman had us some hard words.'

'It might not be him,' Ella objected. 'Kate couldn't say definitely.'

'That's all right, ma'am. Happen I'm wrong. I'll apologise.'

'Would you take some food before you go to the jail?' Ella asked, watching the Ysabel Kid and knowing that he was probably the most dangerous of this hard-faced trio, the most deadly man she'd ever seen.

'Reckon we might as well,' agreed Dusty. 'It's been a fair piece since we last took us a meal.'

Bix Smith looked up as the door opened. His eyes went first to Ella, then to the four men following her into the office. He came to his feet, advancing with his hand held out.

'Cap'n Fog,' he whooped. 'I knowed you'd be along as soon as you heard.'

'Now we can likely make us some real war on that Guesthouse bunch,' Simon went on. 'Ole Derry told me he'd send word for you to come.'

'Hush your mouth,' warned the Kid. 'You'll likely be scaring ole Doc off. He don't want no——'

Lynn, who'd followed the others in, snorted. 'Least Doc don't act so mean that he can't afford a cartridge gun and has to tote a cap and ball handcannon and a toad sticker.'

'He's too weak to heft a Dragoon, gal,' answered the Kid.

'What about Waco?' snapped Dusty, in no mood for friendly talk.

'We knows that Waco found the boy, brung him back to home. Then come down here and shed his gunbelt. Then he

116

rode his hoss towards the livery-barn and somebody took a shot at him. His hoss took him over the Colorado, we tried to trail it and lost the line. Couldn't find it again.'

'Who knows he's missing?'

'Just us who're here, Derry, and the men who gunned him,' Bix replied and explained about the letter which Ella produced.

'That ole paint'd've brought him in if he'd still been on its back,' Doc remarked. 'But it wouldn't leave him, happen he fell off.'

Dusty sat at the desk, his face grim and somehow he suddenly appeared to be the biggest man in the room. 'Tell me everything that happened,' he ordered. 'Right from the beginning.'

Bix began to tell his story of Waco's arrival and everything that happened after it. Dusty and the others never said a word, their eyes on the old man's face. Not until Bix lifted the Gatling gun magazine from the desk drawer and laid it on the top before them, did any of them show any interest. They all looked down at the round drum magazine, then at each other.

'Von Schnabel came in a couple of days back told us he'd lost this, we didn't say as how we'd found it though. Allowed it was offen an old Civil War Gatling he bought for his firearms collection,' Bix remarked.

'This wasn't off any Civil War model,' Dusty replied. 'It's one of the new Accles Positive Feed Magazines. Only the newest models use them.'

'What'd he want with a new Gatling gun?' asked Bix.

'Don't ask me. Down nearer the Mexican line he might have sold it to some bandit, or revolutionary. He couldn't sell it up here and wouldn't need it to defend his place, there's no hostile Indians hereabouts.'

'Talking about Injuns,' Simon remarked. 'That boy young Waco went to find, he's been saying he saw him eight Injuns and an old buffler-hunter crossing the Colorado river. I talked to him, way he described 'em I'd say they was Apaches, but I never heard of Apaches this far north.'

'Eight!' Dusty drawled, but he sat straighter in the chair. 'We called in at Fort Reynolds, got a friend in command down there. He told us that damned near every Injun reservation's been losing a few bucks for a spell, they'd be gone for maybe a month or more, then show again and not tell where they'd been. Not just ordinary bucks, but the worst kind of white-haters, real badhats. Just before we left there, the Mescalero reserve by Reynolds lost eight of their worst badhats. Really lost them. The Kid tried to find their line but even he couldn't.'

'Then you reckon——?' Ella began.

'I don't reckon nothing at all, ma'am,' Dusty answered. 'They could have gone below the border to join one of the badhats.'

' 'Cepting what that ole squaw kept telling us about an old white buffalo-hunter,' put in the Kid.

'Where at's this boy now?' asked Dusty.

'Likely at school, down by the livery-barn,' replied Bix. 'Want for us to go along with you, Cap'n Fog?'

'Sure,' agreed Dusty, glancing to where Doc and Lynn were talking by the door, oblivious of the others. 'If ole Doc can spare us the time, that is.'

'Don't you have any romance in your soul, Dusty?' asked Mark, eyeing the blushing pair.

'He just don't have a soul,' growled Doc.

'Looks like you've got some trouble coming up,' said the Kid, moving to the window and looking out.

The others joined the Kid and looked at the big crowd which was approaching the jail. There appeared to be a good cross-section of the community present; well-dressed townsmen, gamblers, working people, cowhands, various other kinds of people less easy to define. They were led by a square-shouldered tall man, wearing gambler's clothes but who bore himself like a soldier. Dusty saw something more. Wharton and two men were coming from the side door of the Guest-house, they looked towards the crowd, then headed for the Twin Bridge Saloon.

'Lon,' Dusty said, his voice low and urgent. 'Get down to the Twin Bridge, fast. Wharton and two more are headed there. Likely they aren't after soft drinks and gentle words.'

'Likely they'll get one or the other,' replied the Kid and left the jail by the rear door.

'Can the Kid handle it alone?' Ella asked worriedly.

'Happen he'll get help, ma'am,' Dusty replied. 'I've heard some about those girls of yours.'

'Who's the gent leading the parade?' Mark asked. 'Powerful important he looks.'

'That's Von Schnabel, the man we've been telling you about,' Ella replied. 'I didn't know he was in town today.'

'Looks like he is, and got him a tolerable bunch of friends along to see he gets his way.'

'Not all friends, Dusty,' replied Ella. 'Some of them are my friends.'

Bix Smith and Simon Girty stepped from the office and on to the sidewalk, looking politely down at the crowd.

'These good people have come to see justice done,' Von Schnabel announced.

Some of the 'good people' looked distinctly worried as they saw the three Texas men who followed Bix and Simon out of the office. Behind Von Schnabel, the two madames stood looking up with worried eyes.

'Was justice done half of these *good* people would likely be in jail,' said Dusty dryly. 'Howdy, Bonnie, haven't seen you in a coon's age.'

'Told you not to back Earp and the Law 'n' Order Party in Tombstone, Bonnie,' Doc Leroy went on. 'Knowed they'd run you out if things got rough.'

Von Schnabel snorted, not wanting the business on hand to be forgotten in idle chatter. He did not know who the three men were, but his eyes went to Dusty and gave him a long, hard look.

'This man'—he indicated a soberly dressed little man behind him—'is a Mormon. He saw some of his cattle butchered and followed the men who did it. Saw them hide the hides of the cattle in the woodpile behind the ranch they work on.'

'Which ranch?' asked Bix Smith grimly.

'The BM.'

Dusty heard Ella's startled gasp and wondered if the woman had some connection with the ranch. He looked at the Mormon and asked, 'You sure of it?'

'He followed them,' replied Von Schnabel. 'I want to know what the law is going to do about it.'

'What'd you want doing?' asked Bix.

'We have a sheriff who is never in town, has not been since the day of the election. I want to know where he is.'

'You saw the letter.'

'I saw a letter, deputy,' agreed Von Schnabel. 'I also know that Drifter Smith hasn't showed up at any ranch in the county. So all these good people have joined with me to demand that Drifter Smith either returns by Saturday or I be given the sheriff's post in his default.'

'Now hold hard there,' Trenard, the storekeeper, growled, moving forward. 'There's some of us don't go on that at all. We allow Drifter knows what he's doing all right.'

'Say, howdy, Grenville,' Mark Counter's eyes picked out a fattish gambler who'd been trying to hide in the crowd. 'Are you one of these here good people? Why, I tell you, ole Just Smith and Brit won't never believe it when I write them.'

The man, who was no longer known as Grenville, licked his lips nervously. He started to force his way through the crowd, headed for the hotel to collect his belongings. If the two men mentioned learned where he was they'd be likely to come and call on him. He didn't aim to be in Two Forks when they came.

'What'd you want us to do, Mr. Von Schnabel?' asked Bix politely.

'Go to the BM, investigate and arrest, if you find the hides.'

The German was pleased with this plan. Bix Smith and Simon were friends with the BM crew and if they refused could be suspended from office, allowing two of his own men in. If they agreed, Bix and Simon would find proof and there would be trouble. Even if the skins were not found at the BM ranch for any reason, there were still the BM hides at the Mormon place. That would blow up into a range war instead of bringing about the arrest of the BM's owner. Any way it went, Bix Smith was in the middle and would have to admit he did not know where Drifter Smith was.

'Sure we'll bring the BM in,' drawled Bix. 'Need us some more men to handle it though. The BM runs a tough crew.'

'You may use as many of my men as you need,' offered Von Schnabel.

'Couldn't deprive you of them. Thanking you, most to death for the offer,' replied Bix. 'See, these three cousins of me 'n' young Drifter's just arrived. I'll take them with me. Dusty, Mark and Doc Smith.'

'Smith!' Bonnie snapped out. 'You reckon I don't know Dusty Fog, Mark Counter and Doc Leroy when I see them?'

'Whaal, Smith's their mother's name,' answered Bix. 'They'll take on for me.'

'Why those three?' asked Von Schnabel. 'They're strangers. We don't know anything about them.'

'Nor us about you,' Mark replied evenly. 'Except that some of the company you keep'd make a hawg stay upwind of you.'

'Who are they?' snorted the German. 'Have they ever been lawmen before?'

The other people of the crowd did not need to ask such a question or need to hear the soft drawled answer Dusty Fog gave.

'We've all been lawmen. Heard tell we were tolerably good lawmen at that.'

'Good enough for me,' Trenard said. 'I was in Quiet Town when you ran the law there.'

'And me,' grunted the old-timer who ran the livery-barn. 'How about you, Banker Cockell?'

'I'm in,' agreed the banker. 'With Mrs. Baker that makes a majority of the County Commissioners in favour. Captain Fog, you, Mark, Doc and the Kid are taken on as special deputies in the absence of Sheriff Smith.'

'Sheriff Smith?' Bonnie said, her face lit up with sudden inspiration. 'I know who Drifter Smith is now. He's that tough Arizona Ranger, Waco, we've been hearing about.'

'The one the Pinkerton Agency is looking for?' Von Schnabel put in, seeing a chance to get rid of the sheriff. 'A wanted man?'

'And what he's wanted for,' whooped Trenard. 'Just let any damned Pinkerton sneak come here after him.'

There was a mumble of approval, for most of the crowd agreed that Captain Mosehan, Waco and Doc Keroy should be given the highest praise for their actions in the capture of the murderer Chacon. More than ever the young sheriff's stock in the town rose.

'All right,' Dusty snapped, cutting down the crowd's talk. 'We'll bring in the BM crew, then we're going to make the rounds of this town. We're going to check every wheel, deck and dice. This town's going to get a clean out.'

'You can't get away with that,' a sullen-looking man yelled. 'This ain't Brownton and Mulrooney in Kansas.'

'Mister!' Dusty's voice dropped to a gentle drawl. 'It's not. You ran out of Brownton when we came. Let's see if you're any braver now.'

The man licked his lips. He carried a Remington Double Derringer in a trick sleeve hold-out, guaranteed to give him below the half-second in speed. He did not mean to give it a try-out against a man who could draw and shoot a Colt with either hand in under the half-second.

'I'm not facing to a gunslick like you——'

Dusty came from the porch, his hands bunching the man's coat lapels and shaking him hard, then shoving him back.

'You wouldn't stack against any man who wasn't half drunk on the snake-poison you call whisky. Either clean up your place or get out.'

There was a low rumble of approval from the better class citizens of the crowd, for the man's place was the most crooked in town since Dillis left. The saloon-keeper staggered back, he turned and stumbled away, his face ashy white. He was on the afternoon stage out of town, leaving behind him his saloon but satisfied to be going with his life.

'I just saw that Beth Morrow coming into town,' a man said, coming from across the street. 'Makin for the livery-barn with two of her hands.'

Von Schnabel nodded to the man, one of his crew. The man knew Beth by sight, but had never seen the young Texan they called Drifter Smith, so did not know him.

'Get me a badge, Bix,' Dusty ordered. 'I'll go and bring them in.'

Bix went to fetch the deputy badges for the three Texans. Dusty pinned his on and felt Ella's hand on his sleeve. The woman looked almost sick with worry.

'Dusty, go easy. Don't hurt the girl. She's not done anything wrong.'

'No, ma'am,' replied Dusty. 'I'll ask her to come in.'

The crowd started to follow the deputies along the street. Lynn came to her mother's side, looking at her face. 'What is it, maw?' she asked.

'Nothing. Come with me.'

With that, Ella started after the others and Lynn followed her mother, shaking her head and feeling worried, for she'd never seen Ella so perturbed.

The crowd saw Dusty turn the corner to make for the rear of the livery-barn. Dusty and Mark walked side by side, with Doc just behind them. They came around the corner and Dusty yelled, 'Waco!' His hands crossed, bringing the matched guns out in a flickering blur of movement.

The Ysabel Kid left the jail by the rear door, cut through the space between it and the next building, and headed for the Twin Bridge Saloon. Even as he went along the street he saw men leaving the saloon and made better time. He came on to the sidewalk and looked through the window. The girls were all backed into one corner, except for Molly, who lay on the floor, and another girl who was held on the table by the two gunmen while Wharton gripped her hair in his left hand, his right holding the bowie knife.

'Where is she?' snarled Wharton.

The Kid's old Dragoon came out and he kicked open the doors, coming in fast with a Comanche wild yell of 'Wharton!'

The two men let the girl free and started to turn, hands fanning towards their guns, while Wharton stood as if rooted to the spot. The Kid's old Dragoon bellowed out like a cannon and one of the gunmen was flung backwards by the round, soft, lead ball. The second man's gun was almost clear when he caught a bottle, hurled at him by Big Madge. The woman's aim was good, the man spun around and crashed to the floor.

Wharton's left hand made a move and the Kid's old Dragoon lined on him.

'Pull it, Bengeeman,' came the words from the savage Dog Soldier's mask which the Kid's face now resembled. 'Just pull it.'

Wharton did not aim to do anything foolish. He knew the Ysabel Kid, knew how little regard for human life that dark boy possessed when he was good and riled. The hand came well clear of his gun.

'He's the one who shot Drifter Smith,' Madge called from

the bar, coming around it and advancing. 'Told us so, and Kate talked when she come round for a spell.'

The Kid's Colt revolved on his finger and went back to leather. 'Guns or knives, Wharton?' he asked. 'You've got to choose one or the other.'

Wharton looked at the Kid, knowing how little chance he stood against the Kid with either gun or knife. There was no way of avoiding a fight, no chance of throwing himself on the Kid's mercy, for Loncey Dalton Ysabel felt no mercy for the man who had gunned down his friend.

'Knives it be, Kid,' he croaked, there was always a chance he might be able to draw a gun when the fight started.

'Throw your guns in the corner then,' said the Kid gently. 'Do it any way you feel like. I don't trust you.'

Wharton gulped. He lifted the guns clear but once more he found himself lacking what it took to try and use them. He threw the guns into the corner of the room, then looked at the Colt by the Kid's side.

'You're still wearing your guns, Kid,' he objected.

'Why sure,' agreed the Kid. 'I trust me.' For all that he drew the gun and offered it to the girl. 'Here, ma'am. First man that comes through that door who isn't me—use it.'

While Big Madge was still trying to work that one out the Kid was drawing his bowie knife. With a wild yell that was half fear Wharton hurled forward; he ignored the sawed edged bowie knife at his belt, bringing up the wicked Arkansas toothpick from his boot. He attacked with speed, hoping the treacherous move would take the Ysabel Kid completely by surprise.

The Kid's reaction came Comanche fast, came with the knife skill of the greatest cold steel experts of them all. The bowie knife caught and deflected the narrow Arkansas toothpick, sending it to one side. The toothpick was a knife which could only be used for stabbing, a murderer's weapon. The bowie knife drove out, Wharton saw it flickering towards him, desperately tried to parry the slash then felt it bite in just over his waistbelt. A numbing pain welled through him and he pitched to the floor.

Stepping back, the Kid looked down at the writhing body, wiped his knife blade on his hand, then sheathed it.

'Sorry to muss up your floor,' he said mildly to Madge, who was looking pale and ready to fetch up over the floor. 'Get your swampers to tote these three out and don't let any of your ladies touch Wharton. He won't look pretty.'

Madge returned the Kid's Dragoon to him. She gently kicked her unconscious victim in the ribs. 'Not this one. We girls aim to have a talk with him when he's able. We'll teach him not to come here abusing poor, defenceless ladies.'

The Kid grinned back at the woman, holstered his gun, set his hat right and drawled, 'Kick for me, ma'am.'

Then he walked from the saloon with no more concern than if he'd just taken a meal.

CHAPTER THIRTEEN

BETH MORROW MEETS HER MOTHER

BETH screamed as Jack Hatch started to draw his gun. From the corner of her eye she saw three men come around the corner, saw the flickering blur of movement as their hands went down and heard the yell of 'Waco!' Then shots were roaring from the guns the three men drew.

Jack Hatch's gun was almost clear of leather when he was thrown backwards by the smashing impact of five heavy bullets. He was dead before he hit the ground and it was later found that any one of the five bullets would have killed him.

Waco shook his head, glanced briefly at the girl, then gave a yell.

'Dusty, you old lobo!' he whooped and leapt forward with his hand held out.

Beth let out a gasp of joy, Texas' memory has returned. He knew who he was and she knew who he was also. The name of Waco, the Arizona Ranger, had reached Two Forks County. He was a man any girl could be proud of. If was not until Waco was shaking hands with the three men who saved him that she remembered the Navy Colt by her side.

The girl appeared to be in a daze, she barely noticed the people who were crowding through the alley towards the corral. Texas had his memory back, he was a man to be proud of, the way was clear for them to think about—— Fear, cold fear gripped her. Would he now remember her?

She saw him turn, saw his smile and the way he looked at her, then heard him say, 'Boss-lady, I want you to meet——'

The rest of the words ended as she raced forward to throw her arms around his neck and kiss him.

'Now how do you reckon he does it, Dusty?' a drawling voice asked.

'Why, I tell you, Mark. It's a sure enough mystery. Anyways you're the expert on women and love.'

Waco gently moved the girl back to arms' length, watching the laughter and tears on her face. He saw his three friends standing by with tolerant smiles.

'Boss-lady,' he said. 'I'd like you to meet my good friends, Dusty Fog, Mark Counter and Doc Leroy.'

She took each hand in turn, eyes going to the great spread of Mark's shoulders and thinking he was nearly as handsome as her Texas. She could hardly believe this small, insignificant-looking man was the Rio Hondo gun-wizard, Dusty Fog; until she remembered how fast his guns had come out. Doc Leroy looked a pleasant young man and worthy of having Texas' friendship.

'Who was he, boy?' asked Dusty.

Waco gently moved the girl to one side and joined the others by the side of the body. Beth stood alone; Johnny had moved forward to get a chance to say he'd talked with the Rio Hondo gun-wizard, Dusty Fog.

Ella and Lynn came through the crowd. Beth saw the other girl and licked her lips worriedly. Her conscience had been pricking her ever since the fight and she wished to apologise. She stepped forward to confront the other girl.

'I was hoping to see you,' she said.

The words were badly chosen. Lynn looked at the other girl, looked down at the holstered gun and read the wrong meaning to the words. Her hand lifted over the butt of her Colt Lightning and she said, 'All right, girlie, start any time.'

Beth felt anger surge up. She'd offered the olive branch and got slapped in the teeth with it. She aimed to show this saloon girl that she was not the only one who could use a gun. Her hand lifted, hot anger filling her.

Ella lunged forward, her face suddenly old and strained. She caught the girls by the arm and pushed them against the livery-barn wall.

'Beth, Lynn!' she gasped. 'Stop it, both of you. Stop it before you do something you'll regret for the rest of your lives.'

'Let me go!' Beth answered.

'No!' Ella's voice was hoarse. 'Lynn, this girl's your twin sister.'

The girls stopped struggling, their faces losing all colour. Lynn stood without a move, but Beth staggered against the wall, her legs weak as she stared at Ella's face.

'Sisters!' Lynn gasped. 'You mean she—I—we——!'

'It's true! So help me, it's the truth,' Ella replied, and the girls could hardly doubt her. 'I wouldn't go with your father when he went to ranch in Wyoming, Lynn. So he took you with him. I let my sister and her husband take you, Beth. I worked in saloons and couldn't have kept you. I kept you supported and when you were too old to remember anything about me I bought the Twin Bridge Saloon here, to be near you and keep an eye on you.'

Beth started, tears shining in her eyes. So many things were coming clear to her now. 'But why didn't you tell me?' she gasped, looking first at Ella, then at Lynn, noticing the like-ness between the three of them for the first time. 'All this time you've been in Two Forks and never told me. That's why Seth always came to see you when he was in town, to tell you how I was. That's why I'd see you looking at me when I was in town or at dances. I never knew. Why didn't you tell me?'

'I own a saloon,' replied Ella, not daring to look at the girl.

Lynn stood by her mother, hand on her arm. She was willing to accept her new sister, give Beth love, affection, but only if the question was answered right.

Beth's face was alight with emotion. Pride in this woman who'd done so much for her and was willing to live away from her rather than chance spoiling her life. She tried to speak, then the words came pouring out.

'The best, straightest, squarest saloon in the West. You thought I'd be ashamed of you because of how you make your living. Why should I be. You run a decent place and I've always been taught that the decent saloons are all right. I'm not ashamed at all, mother. I——' She paused to try and show her new-found mother how proud she was. Her eyes went to Waco and the other Texans who were, with the rest of the crowd, standing listening to this new and dramatic develop-ment. She could think of no better way of showing her mother the trust she felt than by introducing the man she meant to marry. 'Texas,' she said, 'I want you to meet my mother and sister.'

Talk welled up through the crowd, excited talk which was brought to an end by Dusty Fog moving towards the crowd.

'These folks want to talk thing out,' he said pointedly. 'Back off on to the street and let them get on with it.'

There was no question of a request now. Dusty Fog was giving orders and not one of the crowd, not even Von Schnabel, thought of arguing.

Ella stood looking at the two girls with tears in her eyes. She saw the significance of the girl's action, introducing this man who obviously meant so much to her. Beth was not ashamed of her, was willing to accept her and had called her mother.

Lynn took a lot of getting down. She grinned at Beth and hugged her. 'I kept thinking when I was licking you down at the saloon, that you was tough for a milk-faced town gal.'

'Licking me?' Beth replied, hugging Lynn back. 'Is that what you call the hiding I gave you?'

'What're you doing with Drifter here?' Lynn went on, suddenly realising that a dead man stood before her.

'Drifter?' Beth gasped, staring first at Lynn, then at Waco. 'But he isn't Drifter Smith.'

'He surely is, sister-mine,' Lynn laughed.

'He's our sheriff,' Ella explained. 'I don't know how you came together, but he's our sheriff.'

'It's a long story, boss-lady,' Waco smiled, slipping an arm around her shoulders. 'I'll tell it you as——'

At that moment Von Schnabel returned, followed by a good portion of the crowd, including the Mormon who was supposed to have seen the butchering. The German strode forward to halt before Waco.

'So, you have returned, sheriff,' he said. 'Good! You will now arrest Miss Morrow for butchering Mormon cattle.'

'Why, you——!' Waco began, moving forward while Johnny folded his fist.

Mark Counter's hands shot out, gripping the two younger men by their belts and holding them without any apparent effort. 'Simmer down there,' he said.

'Why, surely so,' agreed Dusty. 'You'd best take the lady in, boy. There's proof to what this gent says.'

Waco was quivering with rage. He stared at Dusty, hands

clenching and unclenching in anger.

'This man brought certain proof, sheriff,' Von Schnabel went on. 'He followed the BM men and saw them hiding the steer hides in their woodpile. So you must arrest Miss Morrow pending a full investigation.'

Lynn flung herself forward, between Dusty and the German, her eyes blazing in fury as she reached for her gun. 'Why, you lousy——!' she began.

Her hand slapped down on to an empty holster. She turned fast and found Dusty held her gun. There was a look in his eyes which ended her angry outburst.

'Look, ma'am, this's for the law to handle. You just stand back there afore I slap you in a cell for disturbing the peace.'

Before the fuming girl could speak she felt a hand catch her arm. Doc Leroy hauled her back, his face grim.

'You try it again and Dusty won't have to. I'll do it myself and tan your hide with a razor strop.'

Ella expected an explosion, but Lynn looked contrite and behaved herself. A smile flickered across her face. It looked like her family, already double its size since the morning, might be growing even larger very soon.

'It's like this, Waco,' Dusty went on. 'This Mormon gentleman came here to make a report about the BM butchering his stock. Got him real good proof of it, looks like. So, being a good, tax-paying citizen he expects the law to do something for him, and these public spirited folks are here to see it does.'

Waco opened his mouth, then closed it again. He'd complete trust in his friend Dusty Fog but could not see what Dusty was getting at.

'What do you want me to do?' Waco's voice was brittle and harsh.

'Ain't but one thing we can do. Hold this lady until we've been out to her place and looked into the butchering business.'

Bix Smith was scowling at Dusty. Johnny and Simon looked disgusted and were both contemplating seeing if he was as fast with a gun as they'd heard he was. Lynn was almost purple with rage, while Ella and Beth stood side by side and looked as if they couldn't believe their ears.

'Where's the County judge at, ma'am?' Mark asked Ella.

'Out at his ranch. He won't be in today.'

'Then send for him. Make sure he realises how important it is to hold this hearing,' Dusty suggested, never taking his eyes from Ella's face. 'We'll have to hold Miss Morrow.'

'No you won't,' yelled Lynn. 'My sister's not going to jail.'

'Ain't none of us'd feel the need for that, gal,' replied Dusty, turning to Von Schnabel. 'Now is there, mister?'

The German saw that he was driven into a corner. He could hardly suggest that a girl like Beth be held in the jail, that would turn a whole lot of his support away from him.

'No. It would hardly be right.'

'We'll release her in her mother's care,' said Dusty. 'I reckon you'll guarantee her arrival for the hearing, Mrs. Baker, ma'am?'

Ella nodded. She was almost too dazed to speak. 'I will.'

'Miss Lynn, I'll deputise you to take care of your sister. Doc, you go with the ladies and wait for us at the jail. You'd best have your gun back, seeing as you're a deputy.'

Lynn snatched the gun from Dusty's hand, giving him a look which clearly said she hoped it burned his fingers off. Then she opened her mouth to make some blistering remark but Doc pushed her gently and told her to move off.

The two girls walked through the crowd, followed by Doc, and slowly the people separated to go about their business. In some cases the business would consist of straightening out crooked gambling gear ready for the forthcoming check-up.

'All right, boy,' Dusty said to Waco after the crowd had gone leaving only friends near to hand. 'Call me down before you swell up and bust.'

Waco let his breath out in a long rush. 'Dusty, had it been any other man but you I'd have killed him. That gal's innocent. I know all about the hides.'

'Why sure, boy,' agreed Dusty. 'But that don't mean you've got to start in to flapping your big ole mouth off about it afore the public-spirited gentleman, now does it?'

Mark laughed. 'You allus did talk too much, boy. Now you just tell us all about it, while we walk down to the jail.'

Waco took Ella's arm, gave it a gentle squeeze and started to walk her towards the jail. He told the others all that happened to him, seeing more of the picture now he could remember who he was and what occurred.

None of the others spoke as he finished, then Mark looked, down at Waco's sides and smiled. 'You're a fine sheriff, boy. Going out without your badge or your guns. Didn't you learn anything from us?'

'Nothing useful,' replied Waco, then looked at Ella. 'You're looking a mite peeked, Mrs. Baker, ma'am.'

Ella shook her head as if to clear it. Her face was radiant and happy as she looked at him.

'What a day. I nearly see my two daughters shoot it out with each other. Find that Beth's proud of me and that I'm likely to be having a son-in-law or two real soon. Then see one of my daughters jailed for butchering cattle. And I still like the world.'

'Would you mind having a son-in-law, ma'am?' asked Waco.

'No. I think you'd make Beth a good husband.'

'One thing, ma'am, afore you start planning the wedding,' Dusty put in. 'How well do you know the Judge?'

'Which means would he do me a favour, I suppose.'

'Yes'm. That's just what it means.'

'I think he might.'

'I want him to be too busy to hold the hearing until the end of the week, ma'am,' Dusty said. 'By then we should have the right men; happen Waco called it right they're at Von Schnabel's ranch.'

'I think he'd arrange it,' Ella replied. 'Will Beth be all right?'

'The only way she could get hurt is after I'm dead,' Waco answered. 'What you fixing to do, Dusty?'

'Fetch those skin-hunters in.'

They reached the jail and entered. The Ysabel Kid came to his feet, his hand held out to Waco. 'Waal, I'll be damned,' he said. 'And I just had words with poor ole Bengeeman Wharton over killing you.'

Waco gripped his friend's hand in a crushing grip. 'I hope you warn't too rough on him.'

'Was he a nicer man I'd go to boothill 'n' apologise.'

'What happened down there, Lon?' asked Dusty.

'Him and two more were fixing to get the gal we took from the Guesthouse. I had to shoot one, the other was knocked down by a well-throwed bottle. Then me'n old Bengeeman took to discussing which was the best, an Arkansas toothpick or a real genuine James Black bowie: said James Black bowie taking the day. When I left, some of the ladies was taking the last of them *hombres* out and cooling his brow with soft hands and gentle words.'

Ella could almost feel sorry for the man and doubted if his own mother would recognise him when the three big bartenders got through with him.

Lynn stood protectively by the other girl. 'If you think my sister's going in a cell to please you——!' she began.

'Hush your mouth, woman,' Doc put in.

'I'll hush your fool head for you!' Lynn yelled back at him.

Waco went to Beth and gently laid a hand on her shoulder. 'Don't you worry, boss-lady. Dusty acted for the best——'

'Best is it?' Lynn screeched. 'That short-growed towhead should be——'

'Lord save me from angry women,' groaned Dusty. 'They're wuss'n a steer fresh pulled from a mudhole. If we hadn't arrested Miss Morrow, that fine upstanding public-spirited citizen'd started yelling about the law playing favourites.'

'Sure and Dusty fixed it so that same citizen couldn't have Miss Morrow all locked up in a cell,' went on Mark. 'Which same's something.'

'So's toothache,' yelled Lynn. 'And I don't like that either.'

'Ole Doc there pulls a mean tooth,' Mark told her.

'There can't be one law for one and one for another, ma'am,' Dusty put in, before the spluttering Lynn could say another word. 'Not the way I've always been taught to play it.'

'Say, Bix,' Waco suddenly said. 'What happened to them five stage hold-ups I brought in?'

'They escaped,' Bix replied. 'Snuck out the night you took your ride.'

'Don't you worry none over it,' Waco drawled. 'I'd bet I know where to get hold of them again.'

Dusty looked at the two girls, his eyes dropping to Beth's side. 'Fine pair of deputies your pair turned out to be,' he told Lynn and Doc. 'Your prisoner's still toting her gun.'

Lynn laughed. Now her new-found sister was in no danger

of being shoved into a cell she was willing to be friends.

'I tell you,' she remarked, taking Beth's gun. 'If I thought bad things about Dusty, there's only one thing I can say—they were all true.'

'What do you mean to do, Dusty?' Ella asked.

'Like I say, we'll fetch the skin-hunters in. Waco knows the lay-out of the Von Schnabel place and he can show Lon a map of it. We'll spend the rest of the day acting normal—or as near normal as the love-struck ones can. Tonight all of us but Doc's going out there.'

The others sat back and listened to Dusty's plans, knowing that he was the master-tactician of them all. Beth, Lynn and Ella watched the men, seeing what made Dusty Fog the man he was.

'Know something, sister-mine?' Lynn asked. 'That lil Texas boy's surely got something.'

Beth sighed, eyes on the man who meant everything in the world to her. She let out another sigh and replied, 'Whatever it is, he got it from Waco.'

CHAPTER FOURTEEN

WACO WINS A BET

THE jail office presented an unusual sight as the county sheriff and his deputies prepared to go on the raid and capture the men who butchered the BM and Mormon cattle.

Waco looked at the other men, he could hardly ask for better backing in this dangerous business which lay ahead. There was Dusty Fog, Mark Counter, the Ysabel Kid, Bix Smith, Simon Girty and Frank Derringer. The latter came along to the jail to meet his old friends and found himself sworn in as a deputy. Doc Leroy was to stay on as town man, holding Two Forks down.

'Let's go in the back and talk things over,' Dusty suggested.

The men went into the room at the rear of the jail and checked over their guns as Dusty went through his arrangements once more, Bix Smith grunted as he listened to Dusty's casual given orders.

'Allow it'll work, Cap'n?' he asked.

'I reckon it might, given luck. We'll be inside the room and you'll be ready to make a real fast come-in when we yell. I reckon we'd——' The small Texan watched the Ysabel Kid rise and make a sign towards the door. Dusty carried on talking in a normal voice.

On silent feet the Kid reached the door and gripped the handle. He wrenched it open, grabbing and hauling inside a man who'd obviously been listening at the outside. The Kid grabbed the man and slammed him into the wall, his bowie knife out under the man's chin, ready to rip home.

'Call your bunkie in,' hissed the Kid.

A second man stepped into the room, his hand dropping towards the side pocket of his coat at the Kid's captive's scared yell.

'Try it,' warned the Kid, 'and your pard'll be talking through a mouth *under* his chin.'

Slowly the man removed a wallet from his pocket, flipping it open. 'We're Pinkerton agents,' he said.

Waco accepted the wallet and glanced at it. He'd seen a Pinkerton man's identification often enough to know it was the real thing. He handed the card back and looked the man over with a scowl:

'All right, so why the spying act?'

Reluctantly the Kid released the man he dragged in and stood back. It was this man who replied:

'We wanted to know who was in here before we came in. Didn't know how we'd stand in with you. A lot of local law don't like us horning in.'

'And I'm one of them,' growled Waco. 'You remember this, and tell Sam Strogoff what I say. Any time one of you comes into my county I want him here to tell me about it.'

'And if he don't?' asked the second man.

'I'll ram his identification right down his throat.'

The two Pinkerton men exchanged looks. They could see that here was one small town lawman who was not impressed by the great Pinkerton Agency. They changed their attitude towards him.

'No need to get riled, sheriff,' the first agent said soothingly. 'We need some help from you.'

'You might even get it. What can we do for you?'

The two Pinkerton men glanced at the watchful group of deputies and hesitated, then one growled, 'It's private.'

'There's nobody here who don't need to hear it.'

Dusty sat back on one of the beds, watching Waco with the pleased and tolerant smile of an older brother. He saw Mark nudge the Kid and exchange grins as they watched Waco work. Dusty did not speak, he let Waco handle it for the youngster was sheriff and Dusty was only one of the deputies.

Thinking back to what Waco was like and what he was like when they first met, Dusty was pleased in the change. Through Dusty's efforts, Waco had turned from a sullen, proddy young gunhand, well on the way to becoming another Wes Hardin or Bill Longley, to a really smart and respected lawman.

'All right, sheriff,' said the man the Kid dragged in. He was a short, thick-set man wearing town clothes, a bulge under his shoulder pointed to a hidden revolver. 'I'm Joe Brone. This's Pete Hamel. We've been working on those big hold-ups that took place over the last couple of years. You know, the 10,000 dollars from the Army Paymaster, the bank in Houston, the mine payroll over to Virginia City. The big ones that we couldn't prove on any gang.'

'I've heard of them,' agreed Waco. 'They were a smart bunch. Were five big ones done by them, wasn't there?'

'We make it twelve. Stretching clear across from New England to California. All big jobs, all showed the same sort of handling and done just like an Army battle every time. We had every man we could on it. Built up the descriptions of the gang who were doing the jobs. Only five men in it. We're near on sure these are the descriptions.'

Brone took out a sheet of paper and passed it to Waco. The young Texan looked down the list, reading the five descriptions and whistling through his teeth. He passed the list to Bix Smith who squinted at it, reading.

'The five you brought in,' he said sorrowfully.

'You've got 'em?' Brone asked incredulously.

'Had 'em,' corrected Bix. 'Somebody done snuck in and took 'em away one night.'

'That'll look good in our report,' sneered Hamel, a big, burly man who wore a loud check suit and sported a short-barrelled Smith & Wesson revolver in his waist band. 'Allen'll be right pleased to hear about this.'

'Mister!' Waco barked. 'I never lose any sleep over what Allen Pinkerton or any of his lousy crew think about me. When you report, just tell Pinkerton that if he'd put these descriptions out instead of hanging on to them to hawg the glory, we might have held on to the five men.'

'Yeah, I reckon we could have played it better,' Brone agreed. 'We haven't had the descriptions for long. It took a lot of doing, checking folks who'd been living in towns where the hold-ups took place, talking to hotel staff, saloon workers. It took us plenty of time to build up these five descriptions.'

'Why come here?'

'Hartley and Graham, the big hardware firm in the east, sold four Gatling guns to a man who had them shipped out west. They were paid for in money taken from the Paymaster robbery. We traced the guns to Two Forks.'

'And you know who got the guns?'

'Nope.'

'Or why?'

'No. Thought it might be for re-sale in Mexico.'

'I'll bet you a hundred dollars even we can get the five men you want, maybe even find the Gatling guns,' Waco remarked.

'Take you,' Hamel promptly replied.

'Time we were going, boys,' Waco said, turning to his deputies.

'You after them five?' Brone put in eagerly. 'We'll come along if you are.'

'We're after a bunch of slow-elkers, first off,' Waco replied. 'You can come along if you like, but it's a County Sheriff's office chore. If you come along you take my orders, without question.'

'All right,' agreed Brone. 'I'll come along under the same rules.'

There were questions seething in Waco's head, he was seeing things more clearly now, even though there were odd strings he could not tie.

The men left the jail, collecting horses and riding out of town. Doc Leroy, in accordance with Dusty's orders, had spread the word that Waco and his men were going to the BM in the night, to take the ranch crew by surprise in the early dawn.

Bix Smith and Simon acted as guides, for they knew the country well. They were skilled performers in the dark and even the Ysabel Kid, who always boasted he never felt happy riding in daylight, could find no fault with the way they moved.

They halted their horses on the rim which overlooked the ranch and all slid down. Now Dusty took command, it was his plan and Waco was willing to allow him to handle it.

'Get to it, Lon,' Dusty said. 'And don't take all night. If they've got any guards out, Lon——'

'Yeah?'

'Use your gun-butt.'

There was a chuckle from the Kid and he was gone, fading into the dark like a shadow. The other men stood in silence although the two Pinkerton agents were clearly annoyed at the delay.

Time dragged by and just as Brone opened his mouth to ask an angry question, the big white stallion snorted and started to move down the slope. The Texans moved after the horse, leading their mounts. Bix and Simon flashed uncomprehending looks at Frank Derringer. The gambler grinned back at them and whispered, 'That ole Nigger hoss's damned nigh human.'

Following the white horse down the slope the men found the Ysabel Kid waiting for them. He jerked his thumb towards the house.

'None of them out that I could find. The house's all locked up and all the crew's in the hawg-pen.'

That figured. A man like Von Schnabel would not give his hired help the run of his house.

'Bix, you, Simon and the two Pinkertons stop here and keep those hosses quiet,' Dusty ordered, holding his voice down.

Hamel growled. 'Who the hell does that small cowhand think he is?'

Simon's grin was full of sardonic amusement as he replied, 'Mister, don't you tell him he's wrong—but he thinks he's Dusty Fog.'

'What're they aiming to do?' inquired Brone.

'Dusty, Mark and the Kid allow to get into the bunkhouse and take as many of the other side's guns as they can,' Bix drawled back. 'That way we get 'em back all alive and talkative.'

'If they pull it off,' sneered Hamel.

'Mister, they'd best pull it off,' growled Bix. 'Most of Von Schnabel's hired guns are in the hawg-pen. They might even have one of them Gatling guns along with them. So Cap'n Fox, Mark'n the Kid aim to try and get them without killing. Going to sneak in and take their guns, which same's why they're wearing moccasins.'

'Powerful lot better than tossing a bomb through the winder,' Simon went on. 'That being you Pinkertons' way, I hear.'

Hamel started to growl out an angry curse but Derringer

silenced him with a grim warning. The Pinkerton men tended to be touchy at any mention of bombs, had been ever since the night in Clay County, Missouri, when Jesse James' mother was injured and his half-brother killed by an explosion. Whether the explosion was a bomb, or, as Pinkertons claimed, harmless illuminating 'Greek Fire' was not certain.

The four Texans went silently down the slope. They were playing a dangerous game, with their lives in the pot and sudden death the price of failure. It was a chance they were more than willing to take. Like four shadows they halted by the bunkhouse door, flattening on either side of the wall. There was no need for further orders for all the four knew what they must do. Waco, reluctantly, was to wait outside, watching from the slit of the door and ready to call the others down when the disarming of the sleeping men was well in progress.

The Kid began to inch open the door, looking in. A lamp stood on the table in the centre of the room, the wick turned down so that there was only a tiny flicker of light from it. This was to enable any man who wished to get up in the night to do so and not blunder around in the dark, waking the others. A man was rolling sleepily from one of the bunks and the Kid closed the door, for he was walking towards it. The other Texans caught the Kid's sign and flattened out on either side of the door, against the wall. The door opened and a man stepped out scratching his stomach in the manner of someone only half awake. Mark moved fast, his right hand Colt coming out, lifting, then slamming down on the man's head and dropping him without a sound to the ground.

'Hawgtie him, boy. Keep him quiet,' Dusty whispered to Waco.

With that, Dusty followed the Kid and Mark into the bunkhouse, halting just inside the room to allow their eyes to grow accustomed to the faint light. Each of them held a length of pigging thong in his hands as they moved forward in complete silence. The ranch crew were sleeping in double tier bunks, their clothing and boots laying on the floor. But their gunbelts were hanging at the bunk ends, ready for easy grabbing if needed.

Halting by the first bed, Dusty lifted the guns from the

holsters and slid the pigging thong through the trigger-guards, making sure the guns did not bang together or make a noise.

It was as Dusty expected. Out on the range these same men would have woken at the slightest sound. Here in the bunkhouse they thought they were safe and were sleeping heavily. There was still danger, however, and Dusty would never have attempted such a thing with lesser men than his two good friends.

For one so large Mark was light on his feet. He moved along the beds facing Dusty, avoiding kicking anything on the floor. He took weapon after weapon, hanging them on the cord in his hand. A man gave a grunt and rolled over in his sleep. Mark froze, hand reaching for the gun holstered at the end of the bunk. He stood without a move until the man settled down again, breathing getting even.

Like a black shadow the Ysabel Kid went the length of the room. This was the sort of work at which he excelled. His long practice at the art of silent movement came from his youthful occupation, just after the Civil War, as a border smuggler. This was a profession which frequently called for silent movement in the darkness. He crouched under the light of the lamp as he went by the table and reached the end of the room. His was the most dangerous part of the business, for he was to disarm both sides of the room, moving forward to meet Dusty and Mark.

The Kid was on the fourth bunk when he felt the gunbelt sliding from the post. He managed to catch it, but there was a slight noise. He saw the sleeper's eyes open and acted fast. The man opened his eyes and might have been excused if he wished he'd stayed asleep. A savage face loomed over him and before his eyes was the eleven-and-a-half-inch, razor-sharp blade of the Kid's bowie knife, ready to slit his throat if he as much as batted an eyelid loudly.

Dusty and Mark saw what had happened and moved along. They doubted if the man dare make an outcry. They worked on, but there was no rush in their actions for they knew speed might lead to noise.

At last the guns were all on the cords and Dusty went to the table. He turned the knob and brought the lamp to full brightness, lighting the room. At the same moment the Ysabel

Kid let out a wild Comanche war yell which was near loud enough to wake the dead.

The men in the bunks woke, grabbing wildly at empty holsters. At the same moment Waco came through the door, guns out. The windows smashed in, Bix Smith, Simon and the Pinkerton men throwing down on the dazed, newly awakened men. While this was happening, Dusty and Mark brought their own guns to bear on the men and the Kid kept his prisoner quiet under the persuasive blade of his bowie knife.

'Lay still, all of you!' Waco shouted. 'The law's here!'

The men in the bunks were awake enough to hear and obey, but not awake enough to make any spontaneous action against the raiding party. All in all it was a very neat piece of work; the men were covered, most of them were without weapons and there was nothing any of them could do.

'Just stay where you are,' Waco ordered. 'I'll get the ones I want first.'

It was certain death to disobey and the men stayed right where they were. The young Texan went along the line of bunks, picking out the small skin-hunter with the missing tooth and six more; there was a seventh, the man who lay outside, guarded by Frank Derringer. Then Waco selected the five hold-up men and as he pointed out each man Dusty came forward, having holstered his guns, to fasten the man's wrists together.

'You got nothing on the rest of us,' remarked one of the men who remained in the bunks.

'Likely,' agreed Waco. 'You got something on your mind?'

'Sure. Turn me and these other boys loose and I'll show you where there's a hell of a lot of guns.'

One of the five hold-up men let out an angry string of words in some harsh-sounding language and lunged forward, only to be caught and held back by Dusty. Hamel looked sharply at the man.

'What language was he speaking?' Waco asked.

'German,' Hamel replied. 'He called this feller a traitor to his master's cause.'

'You'd best show us them rifles, friend,' Dusty said softly.

'Did you get old Walpai Harry?' the man asked. 'I never thought that ole goat'd be ketched in the dark.'

'Who?' Dusty snapped, casting an accusing look at the Ysabel Kid.

'Ole Walpai Harry. He was the skin-hunter, used to fetch the Injuns to see the guns. Never sleeps in the bunkhouse. Allus beds down well from the house.'

'I must've missed him,' grunted the Kid. 'Hell, I knowed I should have rid Nigger in, he might have caught wind scent and let me know.'

'It's no use you worrying over it, Lon,' Dusty answered. 'Waco, take Bix, Simon and Frank, move your prisoners back to town. We'll handle things here.'

'Why sure,' agreed Waco, bending to pick up two cigar stubs from the floor and slip them into his pocket. 'Move 'em out, Bix.'

The prisoners were taken out, horses caught and saddled, then they were hazed off towards the town. Dusty watched them go, then turned to the gunman :

'Show us these guns.'

The man led Dusty and the Pinkertons to a large barn, opening the door. He felt inside the door, found a lamp and lit it. Dusty looked inside, a low whistle coming from his lips. He'd expected a few weapons, but this was more than a few, this was enough to equip a small army. There were cases of rifles, repeaters of various kinds; boxes of ammunition; kegs of gunpowder were stored at one side and in the centre of the room, squat and evil-looking on their tripods were four of the latest model, lightweight Gatling guns.

'Von Schnabel looks like he's a gun-runner,' Brone remarked. 'Where the hell did he aim to get rid of all this?'

'He didn't,' Dusty answered.

'But if he didn't, why the hell did he buy all of it? I'll bet this cost him nearly all the money he took in the hold-ups.'

'He aimed to arm the Indians, give them repeating rifles, Gatling guns. Mister, he aimed to take over the whole United States.'

Brone started to laugh, then he saw Dusty's face and knew the small Texan had never been more serious. 'I don't get it,' he said.

'Nor me,' Dusty admitted truthfully. 'I might even be wrong. I know a soldier, a real Army officer when I see one and that German's all of that. You look at it this way. He gets the badhats from every tribe, shows them these weapons, tells them he'll help them fight us. They'd follow him, likely. And Mister, with these repeating rifles they'd be better armed than the Cavalry. They could take over the west and hold it.'

'You bunch head out,' Dusty went on, turning to the gun-men. 'Don't go near Two Forks, head right out.'

'Hold hard there,' growled Hamel. 'We didn't make no deals with this lot. I want them holding, some of them might be wanted by us.'

'Then get out and catch them for yourself,' said Dusty. 'Drift, *hombres*. Tell Mark and the Kid I said you could go.'

Hamel growled out a complaint but Brone shook his head. The small agent was looking worried. He could see that Dusty might have called the game right. In that case there were more important things than holding a bunch of minor outlaws to see if they were wanted in some part of the country.

Waco brought his prisoners into Two Forks just before day-light. He was contented with his lot. The five hold-up men did not speak all through the ride but the skin-hunters were only too willing to talk. They would tell all they knew and it would be enough to put Von Schnabel behind bars for a long time.

Doc and Lynn were in the office, the girl sat huddled up to him, her head resting on his shoulder and both asleep. Doc woke as the office door opened and he gently eased the girl from him. She groaned, slid her arm around his neck and mumbled: 'Kiss me again, Marvin honey.'

Then she opened her eyes and came to her feet, cheeks flushed, blushing almost as much as Doc. Waco stood grinning at them, but was sufficiently in the same condition to avoid speaking of how he found the two.

'You get them, boy?' Doc asked.

'Why surely not. They got us. Open the cells up and we'll just head in.'

Doc went to the door leading to the cells, opened it and watched the prisoners, still wearing only whatever they had chosen to sleep in, file by him. He put them into the cells, releasing each man's wrists while Waco dumped the clothes he'd brought with him into the cells, for the men to dress.

'Where's Beth?' Waco asked as they returned to the office.

'Down to the Twin Bridge,' Lynn replied. 'She and maw haven't been to bed all night. Me'n Marvin thought they'd want to talk alone, so we come along to the jail and sat here playing cribbage.'

'Yeah,' drawled Waco. 'I saw the cards and scoreboard, right there in the desk drawer.'

Doc glared at his young friend. 'Shucks, that was earlier,' he said. 'I was just trying to get something out of Lynn's eye when you come in.'

'Why sure,' agreed Waco, lifting his eyes to the roof. 'That's the way I saw it, Marvin honey.'

Before Doc could bring out the flustered, riled words which boiled up inside him there was an interruption. The office door was thrown open and Ella came in. There was a bruise on her cheek and Waco knew something was wrong—bad and terribly wrong.

'Waco!' she gasped. 'Von Schnabel's taken Beth. He's got her across at the Guesthouse and he wants to see you.'

CHAPTER FIFTEEN

VON SCHNABEL'S CHALLENGE

WACO caught Ella and helped her to a chair. She saw his face, pale, grim and savage before her and heard his voice, although it was little more than a whisper.

'What did you say?'

'Von Schnabel. He came into the Twin Bridge just now, he and Kyte. I tried to stop them but they knocked me down and Von Schnabel told me to fetch you. He wants for you to come to the Guesthouse alone.'

'Like hell!' Doc snapped, checking his Colt. 'Let's go, boy.'

'No, Doc,' Waco answered. 'They've got Beth. I've got to play it their way. You stay on here, hold them prisoners. Lynn! Get afork Doc's black and head for Von Schnabel's place. You'll find Dusty, Mark and the Kid on the trail. Tell them what's happened here.'

'We'll go with you, Waco,' Simon growled. 'If they've harmed that gal——!'

'They won't have!' snapped Waco. 'But they will if we all go down there. He wants me and me alone, and that's the way he's going to get it.'

With that, the young Texan walked from the jail and along the street through the fast coming dawn. His hands brushed the matched butts of his guns, his feet drove out and down on to the ground. Never in all his life had Waco felt the urge to kill as he did now. If they'd harmed Beth in any way he meant to get Von Schnabel and as many of the others as he could. He reached the Guesthouse, ignored the side door and went along the front boardwalk, halting before the batwing doors. He drew in a deep breath, kicked open the doors and went in, his guns out ready, the hammers drawn back under his thumbs.

Then he halted, the thumbs still holding back the hammers.

Beth was at the bar, Kyte standing behind her. Waco could see the gun which was held close to her side.

'A stand-off, I would say,' Von Schnabel remarked, standing directly in front of Waco's guns.

Waco's eyes went around the room. The girls were all gone, so were most of the workers. Only half a dozen hard-faced, gunhung men remained, and a short, whiskery old-timer wearing buckskins. Not one of them held a gun, they did not need to as things stood.

The young Texan's thumb quivered on the hammers. He could shoot and send Von Schnabel tumbling to the ground but Kyte's bullet would drop Beth in a limp and lifeless pile as soon as he fired. There was nothing Waco could do, he could not risk shooting down the gambler, for the gun at Beth's side was cocked and would fire as soon as the man's finger relaxed on the trigger.

'It's a stand-off,' he agreed. 'I'll holster my guns if Kyte moves away from Beth.'

'I'm sorry, real sorry,' Von Schnabel replied. 'You are so fast that if I did as you say I would be dead before Kyte moved two steps. You will lay your guns on the table and stand well clear of them.'

'If I don't?'

'You will. I am an officer and a gentleman but I would not hesitate to tell Kyte to kill.'

Slowly Waco allowed the hammers of this guns to sink, he laid the matched guns on the table and moved away from them. Von Schnabel picked them up, carried them to the bar and laid them alongside the pair of sabres which were on the polished mahogany top.

'What now?' asked Waco.

'A bargain. You hold my men. I hold something very dear to you. We will make an exchange.'

'Texas!' Beth gasped. 'No. You took an oath, don't break it.'

'You mean turn loose the men I captured and Beth goes free?' asked Waco, playing for time. Hoping for Dusty to come, confident that the small Texan could find some way to break the deadlock.

'Of course. A good officer does not like to leave loyal men

147

behind.'

'How'd you know we'd got them?'

Old Walpai Harry grinned. 'That black dressed boy's real good. Had I been a mite further away I'd have missed him. I woke, saw it was too late to help so I hung around to see what happened, then come back here.'

'I knew that I must get you here, so I took Miss Morrow. I hope Kyte did not hurt Mrs. Baker; a fine woman, a most remarkable woman. I wondered what she had against me, we started on most amicable terms. Then, when I started to plot against the BM she turned against me. I see now that she was protecting her daughter. She had that girl Kate working for me and I never suspected until the clocks were altered. Then I knew there was a spy against me. Even so, she never knew my true plan. She thought I merely wanted to control this small county.'

'And you aimed to control the United States. To arm the Injuns, train them as cavalry. You'd got those Gatling guns. I heard one of them the day Wharton shot me. Didn't recognise the sound at first. I'd never heard a Gatling gun at a distance and didn't get what it was until later,' Waco replied. 'When you had the Gatling guns delivered you lost a magazine. Simon found it. Later, when you found it was gone you told Bix and Simon that story about losing it, buying it for your firearms collection, so that if the magazine turned up they would return it and not bother to check where it came from. Only it was the new magazine, not the old.'

'A shrewd man, a very shrewd man,' Von Schnabel conceded. 'We should have been good partners. With the Indians armed and trained we could have taken all the west. Then we could have swept through the east. There would have been others who'd flocked to our side. When we gained control of the whole country I could have raised the flag of Prussia over the great land and given it to my Emperor.'

'A real smart idea. It'd maybe have been a mite harder than you expected. The Pinkertons were on to you and your gang.'

'Special troop, please,' there was dignity in Von Schnabel's reply. 'The word "gang" implies criminals. My men were soldiers, raiding the enemy. Every cent they captured was put to organising our great coup. Do you know why I wished to be sheriff here, why my men removed the old sheriff?'

'Sure. The county sheriff pulls a powerful load of weight. He's the first man the federal law, the Army or Pinkertons go to when they're investigating anything. He gets a lot of information that he wouldn't otherwise. Besides, as the sheriff you could take control of near on every ranch in the county before you're through. Beth's place bordered yours. You wanted her place to give you more room to train your Indian Army and you didn't want her men riding the range and maybe seeing or hearing something they shouldn't. You reckoned as sheriff and with the county in your pocket you'd have got a good start.'

'That's correct. You're smarter than I thought. Now, about your prisoners?'

Waco looked at the girl. He was a lawman, he'd taken an oath when he accepted the badge and knew that he must go against it. Beth's eyes were pleading with him not to accept. Begging him not to go against his oath, but to stand up to and defy the German.

'You'll never get out of Utah,' he finally said. 'The Pinkertons traced you and your gang. They've given me descriptions of all of them. They traced the Gatling guns to you. There's no way out.'

'A bluff perhaps?' Von Schnabel said gently.

'No bluff, you've got my word on it.'

'Then it is a pity. I will have to take Miss Morrow with me as a hostage.'

'And I thought you was supposed to be a gentleman,' Waco snapped. 'You're no better'n any other yellow owlhoot, hiding behind a gal's skirts when the going gets rough.'

Anger flooded Von Schnabel's face. 'That is an unforgivable insult,' he barked, taking the words as Waco hoped he would. 'Kyte, stand away from the young lady and keep away from her.'

Kyte opened his mouth to object, then shut it again. He moved away from Beth, holstering his gun and watching what was going to happen.

'What now?' asked Waco, looking towards his guns. If there was a chance of getting to them he would.

'As the insulted party I have choice of weapons. I'm not

afraid to admit that you are my master with firearms. I choose sabres.'

'You coward!' Beth gasped, running to Waco and facing the German. 'You low down coward. Taking an advantage of a man like that.'

'Easy, gal,' Waco said gently. 'He's got the choice and I'm as much better with my guns as he is with his swords. Leave her lay, we'll play it that way.'

Von Schnabel took the sabres from the bar, laying one on the table in front of Waco and holding the other. Beth clung to Waco but he gently moved her away from him and smiled down at her.

'Stand at the bar, boss-lady,' he ordered. 'It'll be all right.'

The girl went to the bar and stood watching Waco as he went towards the sabre. Her eyes went to Waco's matched guns, she'd fired a .45 Colt but never with accuracy. She swore that she would try to kill Von Schnabel rather than allow him to harm Waco.

Von Schnabel held his sabre with familiar ease, he watched the young Texan reach for the hilt of the second weapon. 'I wish you were more used to such weapons, sheriff,' he said. 'I hate to think I'm taking an advantage of you.'

Waco picked up the sabre in his right hand. He'd learned a little about sabre fighting in the Rio Hond enough to know how to hold the weapon and do a little work with it. He knew that his little bit of knowledge would be of no use to him against the German.

Slowly Waco hefted the sabre, then his left hand gripped the edge of the table and he threw it full at the other man. Von Schnabel jumped aside, thrown off his balance by the table. He saw Waco leaping at him and parried a fast-taken cut at his side. Waco lunged to one side, grabbing a chair, skidding it at the German and following it with a fast leap. From the street he heard the crash of shots and then was forced to concentrate on trying to get in a position where he could get to his guns.

Von Schnabel was no fool, he knew what Waco meant to do and started a fast attack, driving the young Texan before him. Only Waco's speed and agility saved him from death as he was driven back across the room. His eyes were on Von Schnabel, he could not spare an instant of concentration to see what

Beth was doing.

The girl stood horrified; then she saw that every man in the room was watching the sabre fight and moved slowly towards the matched Colts which lay on the bar. From outside she heard the rapid thunder of approaching hooves, and saw Kyte looking around worriedly. Then she saw Von Schnabel increase the speed of his attack, driving Waco back across the room.

Dusty Fog, Mark Counter and the Ysabel Kid rode slowly towards Two Forks. The two Pinkerton men stayed on at the Von Schnabel ranch to guard the weapons until shipment to town could be arranged.

'Gal coming over the bridge,' the Kid remarked laconically, pointing ahead.

'Looks like she's going places,' Mark agreed, watching the fast approaching rider. 'Hell, that's Doc's black and Miss Lynn riding it.'

Lynn brought her horse to a halt, her face flushed and her eyes wild. 'They took Beth to the Guesthouse,' she gasped. 'Waco's in trouble!'

Dusty and Mark waited to hear no more. They sent their horses leaping forward and the Kid heard the girl's yell. He stopped his white, looking at her.

'What is it, gal?' he asked.

'There's some of Von Schnabel's men watching the bridge and the street,' she replied. 'They're waiting for you to come in.'

'Stick with us, if you can!' yelled the Kid and sent his white leaping forward with a touch of his heels.

Lynn was riding a good horse and she was lighter than any of the Texans but that big white stallion went away as if she was standing still. She caught up with Dusty and Mark but the Kid was already passing them, the white running like a racehorse and the Kid urging it on.

Three men stood at the end of the cattle bridge, two with rifles, the other holding a shotgun. They saw the seventeen-hand white stallion tearing at them, ridden by a figure in white man's clothing, but with the face of a Comanche Dog Soldier. Without slowing his horse, or even breaking stride the

Kid unshipped his rifle. The magnificent 'One of a Thousand' Winchester flowed to his shoulder, his cheek caressed the smooth black walnut stock and his eyes sighted. His first shot tumbled the shotgun toter over backwards. He shifted his aim and sent one of the two riflemen reeling back with a bullet-smashed leg. The third man lost his nerve, and sent a wild shot over the Kid's head, and saw the huge white horse bearing down on him, making the bridge vibrate to the iron shod hooves. He flung aside his rifle and ran for it.

On to Colorado Street tore the Kid. Dusty and Mark were already on the bridge behind him, their Colts in their hands. The Kid came off his horse at full gallop, lighting down on the street ready for action. He went down, rolling over to break his fall, came up and his rifle spat, tumbling a man from cover.

Mark Counter's right-hand Colt came up roaring, and a man staggered into view, clawing at his face, then going down in a heap. The big Texan saw another man leaping from a saloon and shot again, the man stumbled back, went to his knees, then tried to crawl back inside.

A gunman came from the side of a building, his rifle lining on the running Kid. Doc Leroy came through the door of the jail office, his right hand dipped, came up and his Colt threw lead into the man.

Then it was over, silence fell on the street. The rest of the Von Schnabel men called off any attempts at war and started to make for the livery-barn or wherever they stabled their horses.

The Kid whistled and his white came back to him, he went into the saddle as his two friends passed him, joining them as they headed for the Guesthouse. Doc holstered his gun and sprinted along the street, seeing Mark come down from his horse and make for the side door. At the same moment, Dusty whirled his big paint stallion and rode along the boardwalk in front of the Guesthouse. Through the windows he saw what was happening and left his saddle. He crashed through the glass, carrying it and the sash before him. Dusty hit into Waco, knocking him from under the German's swinging sabre. The young Texan felt himself going down, lost the sabre and felt Dusty's Colts thrust into his hands. He rolled over and came to one knee, lifting the guns.

Matt Kyte's Colt was slanting down at Waco when the side door burst from its hinges and Mark Counter stood there. His right hand Colt rocked, the long barrel kicked up and Kyte reeled backwards with a bullet in his chest.

Behind Mark came Doc Leroy and the Kid, guns out, lining on the gunmen before any of them could make a draw. Ole Walpai Harry was the only one to try, his Colt was out and flaming but he missed, for Doc Leroy cut him down.

Dusty came to his feet, holding the sabre and facing Von Schnabel. He could see what had happened and prepared to see how the German stacked against a man who really could use a sabre.

'My pleasure, sir,' said Dusty Fog.

Von Schnabel looked at the small man facing him, saw the faultless stance and the correct way the sabre was held. Here was a man with whom he could match steel, a man who could handle the sabre well. He brought the sword to a salute, which Dusty replied to with a flourish.

Then they engaged blades. Steel clashed against steel as the two men tested each other. It took Von Schnabel just three fast passes to know that he was matched with a man who could really handle a sabre.

Waco ran to Beth's side, catching her in his arms, even while steel rang against steel. He kissed her and then she gasped:

'Stop them, Waco. Stop them!'

'No, honey. Dusty called the play. We've got to leave them as they lay.'

The two men fought with savage skill. There was little to choose between them. Von Schnabel's extra height and reach off-set by Dusty's practice. Where Von Schnabel rarely got a chance to keep his training up, Dusty regularly worked out at the OD Connected, sabre fighting with the other members of the clan, all of whom were good with a blade. So Dusty held just that slight edge over the other man.

The other men watched, although probably only Mark knew much about what was happening. The big Texan was good with a sabre but he admitted that he would not like to face either of the fighting men.

It was a fast action fight. Von Schnabel used every bit of

skill he possessed to take the other man, but he was matched by a skill just as great. Sweat poured down their faces as they battled up and down the room. Both were feeling the tremendous pace and both knew the slightest slip would mean the end of the fight.

Von Schnabel tried to beat Dusty's blade down, making a bind by using the strong edge of the blade, the part nearest the basket hit, to control Dusty's point, or feeble. Dusty parried fast, deflecting the movement of the German's sword. Then, from the half-lunge position, Dusty made his attack.

He brought his weight heavily on to his right foot, swung the left foot forward as far as he could, stamping down hard. His half-lunge changed at the last moment to a thrust.

Too late Von Schnabel saw the flash attack. He tried to bring his own blade into a parry but Dusty's sabre was inside his guard. The point bit into the German's body, driven by the forward thrust until the point came out the other side.

For a moment Von Schnabel stood. The sabre fell from his hands as they clutched down at the blade of Dusty's weapon and he fell to the ground, pulling the sabre from Dusty's hand.

Dusty staggered to a table, leaning against it and gasping for breath. There was not a movement throughout the room as he stood swaying. Then he recovered, got full control of himself, and looked at the others.

'A dead game fighter,' he said. 'Doc, do what you can for him.'

Waco tossed Dusty his guns, then picked up the matched staghorn-butted Colts from the bar and holstered them. He gripped Beth in his arms, turning her from the bloody sight on the floor. Gently he soothed the sobbing girl:

'There now, honey,' he whispered. 'It's all done now.'

Lynn and Ella came through the door and stood looking at Von Schnabel. Doc Leroy removed the sabre and looked up, shaking his head sadly. It was only a matter of time before Von Schnabel died. The man lay on the floor, he spoke in German and none of them could understand it. Then he died.

Dusty looked the hired gunmen over, his eyes cold and hard. 'You lot get out of this town and keep going,' he ordered.

They needed no second telling. They were hired fighting men and the pay ceased with the death of Von Schnabel.

There was nothing for them to fight over any more.

'Got his safe keys here,' Doc remarked, holding a small bunch of keys out. 'Reckon we'd best take a look through it and see what he's got inside.'

'We'll tend to it, *amigo*,' Dusty replied. 'You 'n' Waco best take the girls back to the Twin Bridge Saloon and wait for us.'

CHAPTER SIXTEEN

IF YOU CAN'T LICK 'EM, JOIN 'EM

A WEEK passed after the killing of Von Schnabel, a very busy week for Waco. His telegraph message brought the Territorial Governor hot-foot to Two Forks and started a full-scale investigation into Von Schnabel's affairs. A book in the German's safe, when translated, told his entire plan. How he organised the robberies, using five men who came to America with him, ex-members of his regiment. They planned to use the various Indian tribes as a fighting force and to take over the whole of the United States.

The telegraph wires were busy between Two Forks and Washington, but at the end of the week word came. The United States were not meaning to make an International incident out of the business for the German Government knew nothing of Von Schnabel's plans.

It was a worrying week for Beth. She saw little of Waco, except at the official receptions and formal dinners given for the governor of the territory. Woman-like, she wondered if he was having second thoughts about marriage and settling down, now that he was re-united with Dusty Fog and his other friends.

So it was, one morning she and Lynn stood out back of the jail and watched Dusty, Mark, the Kid and Waco saddling their horses, bedrolls on the saddles ready to ride. Beth was close to tears, for Waco had told her nothing of his plans for the future and she was sure he was riding off with his friends, headed back home to Texas.

'Sister-mine,' Lynn said grimly. 'Was that my fool man riding off with those three fellers I'd haul him out of that kak and stomp on his head.'

Beth shook her head stubbornly. 'If he wants to go, he can. I don't care.'

Waco finished saddling the paint, then looked at the other three. 'You be sure and get back here for the wedding,' he said. 'I reckon another fortnight'll see us clear and give me time to get everything fixed.'

'We'll do it, boy,' Dusty promised. 'We'll fix it with the Arizona Governor to announce an amnesty on you, Doc and Cap'n Burt. Wouldn't want the Pinkertons to try 'n' haul you off to jail on your wedding day.'

'You take care of that lil gal, boy,' Mark ordered. 'You might be sheriff up here but we can still hold you down and "chap" you, if we have to.'

'Surely hates to see another good man go, though,' drawled the Ysabel Kid. 'I bet you she has him all tamed down afore you can say hominy grits.'

Turning, Waco walked towards the two girls. He suddenly realised what he'd done. That Beth was eating her heart out with worry over him. He wanted to take her in his arms and beg her to forgive him. He managed to hold his face straight as he heard Dusty, Mark and the Kid mount their horses.

'Reckon you, Doc and them two ole goats can hold down the town, Lynn?'

'Sure,' replied Lynn, eyeing Waco with cold anger plain on her face.

'Good, then me'n the boss-lady can head out for the spread and have a couple of days in private.'

It took Beth a minute to understand what Waco meant. Then she gave a cry of delight, flung her arms around his neck, laughing, crying, kissing him and gasping incoherent words. The only sensible thing Lynn could make of it was Beth sobbing :

'I knew you wouldn't leave me.'

Lynn watched the three Texans riding away, then turned her eyes to the heavens as her sister and Waco walked towards his horse.

'Lordy me,' she sighed. 'Ain't love just wonderful. If I ever gets that way I hope the sky falls in on me.'

At that moment Doc Leroy stepped from the door of the jail building and stood looking at Waco and Beth. He'd seen considerable of Lynn for the past few days and could tell that she felt the same way about him as he did about her. He slipped an arm around her shoulders and sighed.

'First it was Red Blaze, then Johnny Raybold, Stone Hart, Rusty Willis. Now it's Waco.'

'What're you getting on at?' she asked truculently.

'You know what they say, gal. If you can't lick 'em, join 'em. Will you marry me?'

Lynn flung herself into Doc's arms. Through her excited agreement she saw her mother standing at the door. The girl released Doc and stood with glassy eyes, her face pale.

'What's wrong, Lynn?' Ella asked worriedly.

'Mammy,' replied Lynn happily. 'The sky just fell down on me.'

THE END

Please note that
THE OFFICIAL J. T. EDSON APPRECIATION SOCIETY AND FAN CLUB
will now be operating from a new address

*FREE to members – signed photo of **J. T. Edson**

*Exciting competitions – autographed prizes to be won in every issue of the Edson Newsletter

*YOUR CHANCE TO MEET **J. T. EDSON**
Send SAE for full details and membership form to:

JT Edson Fan Club,
P.O. Box No. 13
Melton Mowbray
Leicestershire

THE QUEST FOR BOWIE'S BLADE *by* J. T. EDSON

The task seemed simple enough to the Ysabel Kid. All he had to do was ride into Mexico, find the man who had killed James Bowie at the Alamo and ask him to return Bowie's legendary knife to its rightful owners. Nothing simpler—or so the Kid thought . . .

But before the job was through he had locked horns with some mighty bad hombres. Men like Manos Grande, the fearsome Yaqui war chief; Silk, a dude but also a lightning fast killer; and Juan Eschuchador, as mean a bandido as ever slit a throat. And then there were the women, real tough ladies like Belle Boyd, the rebel spy working for the US Secret Service or Belle Starr, the outlaw—but at least *they* were on the Kid's side—or were they?

552 09444 7—30p   T180

A SELECTED LIST OF CORGI WESTERNS
FOR YOUR READING PLEASURE

GREAT LEGENDS OF THE WEST

☐ 09147 2　IN THE DAYS OF VICTORIO (illus.)　　　　　　*Eve Ball* 40p
☐ 09095 0　APACHE　　　　　*Will Levington Comfort* 30p
☐ 09098 0　PAINTED PONIES　　　　　*Alan Le May* 35p
☐ 09097 2　VALLEY OF THE SHADOW　　*Charles Marquis Warren* 35p

MORGAN KANE

☐ 09729 2　THE DAY OF DEATH　　　　*Louis Masterson* 30p
☐ 09256 5　HELL BELOW ZERO No. 25　　　*Louis Masterson* 30p
☐ 07274 5　SHANE　　　　　*Jack Schaefer* 30p
☐ 09624 5　COYOTEROS!　　　　*Louis Masterson* 30p
☐ 09388 2　HIGH PLAINS DRIFTER　　　*Ernest Tidyman* 30p

J. T. EDSON

☐ 07840 9　THE REBEL SPY No. 1　　　　*J. T. Edson* 35p
☐ 07844 1　THE TEXAN No. 3　　　　*J. T. Edson* 35p
☐ 08012 8　SAGEBRUSH SLEUTH No. 24　　　*J. T. Edson* 35p
☐ 08064 0　THE TOWN TAMERS No. 31　　　*J. T. Edson* 35p
☐ 08065 9　GUN WIZARD No. 32　　　　*J. T. Edson* 35p
☐ 09113 8　TWO MILES TO THE BORDER No. 70　　*J. T. Edson* 25p
☐ 09650 4　YOUNG OLE DEVIL No. 76　　　*J. T. Edson* 40p

LOUIS L'AMOUR

☐ 07815 8　MATAGORDA　　　　*Louis L'Amour* 40p
☐ 09468 4　THE QUICK AND THE DEAD　　*Louis L'Amour* 30p
☐ 09387 4　THE MAN FROM SKIBBEREEN　　*Louis L'Amour* 30p
☐ 09354 8　LANDO　　　　　*Louis L'Amour* 40p
☐ 08576 6　HANGING WOMAN CREEK　　*Louis L'Amour* 35p
☐ 09264 9　THE FERGUSON RIFLE　　　*Louis L'Amour* 30p
☐ 09191 X　TREASURE MOUNTAIN　　　*Louis L'Amour* 30p

SUDDEN

☐ 09063 8　SUDDEN – GOLDSEEKER　　　*Oliver Strange* 35p
☐ 08812 9　SUDDEN MAKES WAR　　　*Oliver Strange* 30p
☐ 08810 2　SUDDEN – OUTLAWED　　　*Oliver Strange* 30p
☐ 08907 9　SUDDEN – TROUBLESHOOTER　*Frederick H. Christian* 35p
☐ 09170 7　SUDDEN – DEAD OR ALIVE　　*Frederick H. Christian* 30p

All these books are available at your bookshop or newsagent: or can be ordered direct from the publisher. Just tick the titles you want and fill in the form below.

CORGI BOOKS, Cash Sales Department, P.O. Box 11. Falmouth, Cornwall.
Please send cheque or postal order, no currency, and allow 10p per book to cover the cost of postage and packing (plus 5p each for additional copies).

NAME (Block letters) ....

ADDRESS ....

(MAY 75) OP2

While every effort is made to keep prices low, it is sometimes necessary to increase prices at short notice. Corgi Books reserve the right to show new retail prices on covers which may differ from those previously advertised in the text or elsewhere.